To Grace,

It Began With a Letter

Collected Works By

Liz Strachan

With best wishes

Liz

PlashMill Press

Published in Scotland and the United Kingdom in 2009
by PlashMill Press

First Edition

A CIP catalogue record for this book is available from the British Library.

ISBN-13: 978-0-9554535-7-1

Printed by Robertson Printers, Forfar

PlashMill Press
The Plash Mill
Friockheim
Angus DD11 4SH
Scotland.

www.plashmillpress.com

Contents

How It All Began
Letter of Love   2
My Special Day   3

Wartime and Early School
Lizzie's War   6
Post War Playtime   9
Halcyon Days   12
Celebrating One Hundred Years   15

Nature Articles
Table Talk   18
Nuts to Sammy   21
The Life and Times of a Basin Bird   24
The Importance of Being Fergus   27

Teaching Days
Exam Fever   32
DMs for Dancing   34
Ode to Pythagoras   37
School's Out Forever   42
Memories of 35 Years at the Chalk Face   44

Travel
North to Alaska   50
Doing the Strip in Las Vegas   55
A Tourist's Prayer   60
New York New York   62

Researched Articles
A Sinister Way of Life   68
Ten Years Gone But Not Forgotten   73
George Wishart   77
Alexander Burnes   81
Balnamoon's Cave   89

Robert Burns
Ae Fond Kiss   94
Robert Burns Said it First   100

Robert Burns (continued)

Maria Riddell..105
A Most Valued Friend..................................109
Reply to the Toast to the Lassies................114

Women's Short Stories

Computers, Roller Blades and Old-Fashioned Love......118
Valentine Girl..123
New Love on a Friday Afternoon................128
Hot Gossip..132

Poetry

Blue Tit Spring...138

Letters..139

Children's Stories

Sparkle and the Garden Birds.....................148
Daisy's Wishes...151

Funny Stories

Alarming Elsie...156
tryatrio.com...161
The Christmas Adjudication......................167
Old Soldiers Never Die.............................170

Serious Stories

Holding On With Love...............................176
Requiem for Danny..................................182

Other Amusing Articles

Three Go Off to Camp...............................190
The Joy of a Born-Again Gardener.............193
Farewell to the Pound..............................196
Cold Comfort..200
Pensioner on the Piste.............................202
Crazy About Crosswords...........................206
Managing My Mastectomy........................210
Plastered...215

One

How it All Began

Letter of Love

My Darling Little Granddaughter,

Your Daddy phoned me in the middle of the night to tell me of your hasty and very early arrival. He said your weight was only one pound, twelve ounces and I cried. How could such a tiny person survive?

This morning I drove northwards anxious and sad, fearing I might be saying goodbye before we had even met.

But there you were in your incubator, my darling, not only breathing on your own, but crying, showing off to the world that you have healthy lungs. You were dressed in a little pink bonnet and nothing else, and your innocent immodesty allowed me to see that you are perfect.

I stretched out my hand into the incubator and stroked the downy blonde hair peeping out from under the bonnet. I held your tiny hand and your fingers curled round mine in a firm grip as I told you all the family news. Then I wept again, silly grandmother tears of great joy as I marvelled and thanked God for your tiny perfection.

Your eyes are the deepest brown, unusual in a new baby, and you stared at me with what I felt was a look of recognition. With the greatest certainty I knew you were trying to say, "Don't worry, Grandma, I'm going to be alright," and my anxiety changed to a happy peace as I sat with you.

My darling little Lauren, on this special day, I am already dreaming of the fun and the friendship, the laughter and love, that we will share together. God bless you, my tiny first born granddaughter.

With all my love,

Grandma Liz.

My Special Day

One evening in late October 1991, I got a phone call asking to speak to Elizabeth Strachan. I'd had a telesales interruption to my dinner already that evening and I almost put the phone down. I'm glad I didn't.

The friendly lady congratulated me on winning the European Letter Writer of the Year Competition and my prize was to be a luxury holiday for two, staying at the world famous Danieli Hotel in Venice. She wanted to make sure that my husband and I would be able to attend the prize-giving luncheon at the Mirabelle Restaurant in London with overnight stay in the Washington Hotel, first class travel, all expenses paid. A letter would follow confirming all the arrangements.

The letter didn't arrive for another week and meanwhile I worried that maybe it had all been a dream.

Indeed I had almost forgotten that I had entered the competition. Apart from writing newsy letters to friends and helping my two sons with their essays on Hamlet or the romantic poets, I had never written anything since my school days. I was a Maths teacher and was expected only to be a whizz kid in all things to do with numbers.

However the competition entry form had caught my eye, in a jewellery shop in Aberdeen where I was having a new watch strap fitted. It was sponsored by S.T. Dupont, Paris, and fortunately no purchase was necessary.

The subject of the competition was "a letter of love" and I had written that very letter three years before when my first grandchild was born. That secret, emotional piece, welcoming little Lauren to the world was there somewhere in an old diary.

The days before the prize-giving flew by in growing panic. I was interviewed by local newspapers, foreign newspapers wanted my photograph, I had to find the right outfit for the occasion, and my husband and I had to persuade our employers to do without us for a couple of days.

I feared that I would be out of my depth at the luncheon. Well-known literati from TV, newspapers and magazines would be there and all I had written was a 280 word letter. However Maryla, the lovely lady who had first phoned me, guided me through and I even managed an interview for a breakfast television programme. I was able to relax and enjoy the superb luncheon, which ended with coffee and replica S.T. Dupont pens made in chocolate. Thankfully I didn't have to read my letter. The lovely actress, Angharad Rees, did it so beautifully that I noticed a few people, including my husband, wiping away a tear. Then the managing director of S.T. Dupont presented me with a certificate confirming our holiday the following spring.

The week in Venice was the holiday of a lifetime but that day in London was my special time—which will be in my memory forever.

Two

Wartime and Early School

Lizzie's War

(Published in the P&J on 8 May 1995 in a special issue
commemorating 50 years since the end of World War II)

My forty-three year old dad proudly announced that his screaming new four and a half pound daughter was born to raise hell and indeed four months later, Britain was in a 'state of war.' I was small, neat, noisy and fast so the family called me Spitfire. I was at school before I realised that I had actually been christened with the Queen's name.

My memory is hazy about these early years. Some incidents I remember, others I learned from my parents, and over the years I have put them all together like the pieces of a jigsaw falling into place.

I was born at 16, Summerfield Terrace and I lived there for three years. On the night of 25 April, 1942, a German plane dropped a bomb which killed a little girl, the same age as myself, called Sylvia Robertson, who lived only a few yards away at number 22. My Dad, who was on ARP (Air Raid Protection) duty that night, raced home to find every window in the house blown in and my mother and me huddled in a cupboard.

After such a close encounter, we took our ration books and went to live with my grandparents in the safer west end of the city. In the overcrowded tenement house, I was spoilt rotten by four adults and my beloved granny became my best friend and confidante. The only time I can remember not having her full attention was when she was turning the heel of one of the hundreds of socks she knitted for "our brave men." I was blissfully unaware that like many of my contemporaries, I was an undernourished, underprivileged war time youngster.

My mum had many talents. She played the piano, sang like a nightingale and she taught me to read when I was four. But she was a terrible cook and a starving dog would have walked away from what she did with a bit of oxtail. A few months after coupons were required for beef and mutton, other cuts like tongue, heart and head were also rationed, and sometimes the butcher was unable to supply his registered customers with even these disgusting bits. Grandad, who was a gardener, often came home with a rabbit. I would view these furry dead creatures with horror, and my stomach would revolt when my mum brought it, grey and greasy, to the table. At four I was a dedicated vegetarian.

On special occasions, we had a boiled hen. One scrawny bird fed all of us for three days. On the third day, the soup made from the bones looked like stagnant pond water.

My granny was a carrot freak and used them in all sorts of ways. I think she invented the original carrot cake. It was a far cry from the delicious concoction we love today. She made it from dried eggs, dried milk, saccharine, margarine and carrots and she baked it in the temperamental black range oven. If chunks of granny's carrot cake had been dropped over Berlin, Hitler would have come running out of his bunker, hands held high.

Grandad was inventive too. He made me a pair of stilts out of National Dried Milk containers. Before long, every child in the street was stomping around with their feet attached to two tins.

Behind my mother's back, both my grandparents shared their sweetie ration with me. Grandad kept his false teeth in a cup and only wore them on Sundays for going to church. The sermon was always very long and Grandad and I would crunch our way through his two ounce ration of butternuts. Sometimes he would buy motto lozenges and I would consult Grandad about the little homilies like "Love is forever," or, "East, west, home's best," in a stage whisper which distracted the entire congregation.

Under school age children had red and blue Mickey Mouse gas masks but when I went to Mile End School in January 1944, I was issued with the regular version.

Respirator drill was never taken seriously. The boys could blow raspberries through the rubber and we giggled so much that the mica windows would steam up and we staggered round the playground like drunken aliens.

I loved my Class 1 teacher, who was one of the first married women allowed back into the profession. We were an oversized class of war-weary kids whose sleep was often broken by night time sirens and a transfer to the air raid shelters, but Aberdeen children got the best possible education under the circumstances.

The school nurse, Nitty Nora, was concerned that I was so small and thin. "Elizabeth," she would ask, "Does your mother put you through the mangle?" She compensated for the fact that I had never tasted fillet steak, or Stilton cheese or bananas and cream by arranging for me to have an extra bottle of school milk. Eventually with all that milk and an addiction for Strathdee's butteries, I expanded upwards and outwards to her satisfaction.

On 30 April, 1945, the very last air raid warning was sounded in Aberdeen. The news was good and only eight days later, it was all over. We crowded round the wireless with its big acid batteries and listened to Winston Churchill announcing the end of the war finishing his short speech to the nation by saying, "Long live the King!" We all wept with sheer joy.

Life didn't improve immediately. Many men were still in the far east, tragically a few more telegrams would come from the War Office and food rationing went on for several more years.

But on 8 May, 1945, Aberdeen was in party mood. My mum allowed her precious piano to be manoeuvred down into the street. Neighbours found flags and bunting last used for the Coronation and plates, piled high with homemade cakes and spam sandwiches appeared from every house. We cheered and sang and danced until long after midnight and nobody told me it was bedtime.

Soon, at home and at school, the blackout curtains were torn down to reveal a glorious happy summer and for a few years at least, the world was at peace.

Post War Playtime

(This article was published in the P&J 5 November 1993)

During the autumn holidays, I met a group of my pupils. They were fed up, they said, nothing to do. The weather was bad and they had watched too much TV and played too many video games. And now they were looking for something to buy to relieve the boredom.

How different were the long sunny holidays of the post war years. There was no money, no fashionable clothes, no TV, but we were blissfully unaware that we were poor and we were the busiest, happiest kids in the world.

Long after 1945, food was still rationed and in particular, sweeties were in very short supply. Then suddenly it seemed the shops were full. We could only stand and stare! The shop assistant grew impatient as we considered what to buy. Maybe the big penny toffee with its bright and green wrapper guaranteed to extract fillings or even whole teeth at first chew. Or maybe the gobstopper which was exactly as described, a golf ball sized confection which you sucked to reveal a variety of different colours.The only time you could speak if you had a gobstopper was when you removed it from your mouth to see what colour you had got to. Later we graduated to the illicit cinnamon stick, the forerunner of the single Woodbine, and smoked it behind the school bicycle sheds.

Those were innocent times. We knew nothing about violence, crime or drugs. In the school holidays we went off on our bikes to the outskirts of Aberdeen for the whole day with a bottle of tap water, an apple and two doorsteps of white bread sandwiched together with syrup.

We explored the beach, the parks, Rubislaw quarry, the harbour, and we were never warned about talking to strangers. My mother was happily confident that hunger and Uncle Mac's Children's Hour would bring me home at the correct time.

Recreation zones after school were the streets, which in the late Forties were traffic free and safe. There we played rounders and Hopscotch and Cowboys and Indians. We re-enacted the daring deeds of Roy Rogers and Tonto as seen on Saturday mornings at the Odeon Cinema. There was often a bit of friction about who would be a Cowboy and who had to be a mere Indian. The younger you were the more dead Indians you played. Although I was the only girl and the smallest in the gang, I played the Indian role to the limit. I streaked my face with coal and my Mum's only lipstick and wore a gull's feather in my hair and yelled "wa-wa-wa" until they shouted at me, "You're dead, Lizzie!" but I refused to lie down.

Then we swung in the trees in Victoria Park like Tarzan until the park keeper threatened to call the police. I liked to be Tarzan, never Jane. Jane stayed in the tree house cooking for Tarzan. That was not my fantasy.

In Persley Den we cut stalks of hogweed and used them as puffers. With a lung full of air you could fire rowan berries like high speed bullets at bare enemy legs. But in spite of all the killing and wounding that we did, we were happy kids and violence in my life was as unlikely as a trip to the moon.

I suppose I'm making childhood in the post war years seem like a real breeze! But there are one or two things that I still cannot recall without blushing. I loved a boy further up the street with all my ten year old heart. The Co-op milk horse, a creature of habit, used to deposit a large steaming heap on the street outside his door and oh the shame of it, my dad used to go and shuffle it up. Dad's roses flourished but Raymond never invited me to his birthday party.

I spent a lot of time with my grandma who we lived with. She was my best friend and confidante. She was never able to do anything about my dad's mania for manure but she spoilt me rotten and when my parents said "no," I could always rely on my grandma to come up trumps.

She allowed me to listen to the scary "Dick Barton Special Agent" on the wireless, she enhanced my meagre pocket money and she made the best mince and skirlie in the world.

She had snow white hair and wore long skirts with a floral apron on top. She must have younger than I am now. I wonder what she would have said about this granny who goes to work with a brief case and at the weekend wears trainers, leggings and dangly earrings and will never have white hair as long as Boots is in business.

The nearest I ever got to designer label clothes was when my mum got me carefully measured for Clarks sandals. "Size 10" the assistant would declare, so mum bought size 11. By the time I grew into them, it was winter when I had to get boots. The following year the sandals would fit perfectly and the following year my dad cut out the toes so that I got a third summer out of them. My dresses and skirts always had six inch hems to start with. My mother considered that clothes which fitted perfectly at the time of purchase were the height of extravagance. Even my second hand bike had blocks on the pedals for two years!

One of the highlights of my week was when the paperboy delivered the *Film Fun*. I sat at the breakfast table toying with my porridge as I read of the exploits of Old Mother Riley and Laurel and Hardy. Two of my school chums got the *Beano* and the *Dandy* and we swapped so eventually we read them all.

Even in the depths of an Aberdeen winter, you had to be ill before you got a fire in your bedroom. So when I sat up in bed reading to all the hours, I wore a thick knitted cardigan on top of my winceyette nightie, bed socks and yes, woollen mittens.

There must have been some bad days in my golden childhood, days when I was poorly, days when the sun didn't shine, but I don't remember any of them.

Will the children of today remember their discos, Nintendos and Gameboys with half as much pleasure?

Halcyon Days

To be young in post-war Aberdeen was Heaven. They were halcyon days, full of hope, promise and plenty, after the deprivations of wartime.

In schools, the 'jannies' finally removed the blackout curtains and the sun shone into the windows of Scottish education.

In the classroom, discipline was strict. We sat in straight lines, and we all did the same thing at the same time; no differentiated learning in those days! I remember we did a lot of chanting. We chanted the multiplication tables:

"Nine ones are nine, nine twos are eighteen," and so on, day in and day out, until the slowest of us could have been roused in the middle of the night and given, in half a second, the correct answer to 12 times 11.

Then we chanted our history... "Kenneth MacAlpine 844, Kenneth MacAlpine 844." What Mr MacAlpine did in 844 I have never been able to find out. We knew the books of the Bible by heart, Genesis, Exodus, Leviticus, Numbers, Deuteronomy—I was once on a quiz show and was asked: "What is the third book of the Old Testament?" Well, I was the hero of the moment!

We recited the Lord's prayer every morning; "Our Father who chats in Heaven, Harold is his name" ... "And forgive us our trespasses as we forgive them that trespass against us ..." The old lady in the big house next to the school had a notice on her gate, "Trespassers will be prosecuted," so, certain of forgiveness, I raided her garden for conkers of enormous size.

We had a lovely speech teacher called Miss Pugh (unfortunately nicknamed Miss Spew) who attempted to curtail our constant use of the diminutive and take the rough edges off our Aberdeen accents. So we recited 'pomes,' instead of 'po-yums,' and sat with our 'aams' folded, not our 'a-rums,' and sometimes we ate sweets instead of sweeties.

We learned by heart long passages from the 'Golden Treasury,' which although they didn't mean very much to a young girl, have brought joy and comfort to me in later life.

But school wasn't all book-work. Each week I looked forward to our lessons in the gymnasium. We didn't have special kit for PE in those days. We changed into black 'jimmies,' removed our skirts and clad only in voluminous ETB navy knickers and short sleeved white blouses, we cart-wheeled across the dusty wooden floor and scaled wallbars as daunting as Bennachie. Being a bantam-weight, I was the one the gym teacher yanked upside down to demonstrate the handstand and pulled unceremoniously over the leather horse.

What are ETBs? Our knickers had elastic top and bottom, serious elastic which made corrugated red circles on my skinny cod-white legs.

The gym was also the venue for our pre-Christmas Party dancing lessons.

For weeks before the big event we were taught the steps of the reels and strathspeys. Then about the second week of December the excitement grew to fever pitch. The boys lined up against one set of wallbars, the girls on the opposite. When the teacher gave the signal, the stampede began, and you always got the one with the squint or two left feet or Tommy McDonald, who had the early symptoms of a sex maniac. Even this was preferable to being partnered with smelly Robert whose BO made your eyes water.

Those were innocent times. We knew little about sex. Certainly we didn't get sex education at school. We learned about the reproductive system of the salmon and that didn't seem to be much fun as the poor female salmon died after spawning. Nor did we have frank discussions at home about the birds and the bees.

Mavis Carle's sister was a nurse and we pored over 'borrowed' medical books until the whole horrifying picture was revealed. We never did believe that adults could do anything quite so ridiculous.

I loved school but there were some lessons which I was less than enthusiastic about. I hated knitting. I once made a glove suitable for some poor deformed soul with seven fingers. Sometimes I managed to sneak the grubby matted mess home to my mum who picked up my dropped stitches and adjusted the glove to fit a more normal hand.

Even worse than the knitting was the sewing. We made the most horrendous embroidered cotton knickers with double seams in places destined to leave you with serious permanent injury.

Meanwhile the boys were playing football. To be good at football was to put your foot on the first rung of the ladder to fame and fortune. The girls were encouraged to aspire to useful careers like nursing and teaching. It was never suggested to us that we could become captains of industry or professional golfers.

The school was very concerned about our health in these post-war years. Nitty Nora, the school nurse, was a constant visitor.

The 'moving dandruff' was no respecter of heads. Clean or dirty, we all fell foul to the wee crawly beasties. Just when my hair was long enough to wear a ribbon, I had to succumb to the nit comb, the smelly shampoo and the haircut. Poor Robert always had his hair cut to the bone.

I got an extra bottle of milk at playtime as I was particularly small and skinny.

The nurse kept a strict check on my growth and eventually with all that milk and an addiction for Strathdee's butteries I expanded to her satisfaction.

Even as small children, somehow we knew that education was important and that Scottish education was the best of all. Children from every background were regarded as a valuable investment for the future.

I can only wish the same for the children of the Nineties, but somehow I fear these times are gone for ever.

Celebrating One Hundred Years

(This article was published in the Aberdeen Academy F.P. Club magazine, centenary edition 1994)

The evening of 6 May was the first indication that summer might just come to the north east of Scotland this year after all. I told Penny, my hairdresser, where I was going and she made a vain attempt to turn back the clock thirty-eight years. However, with the sun shining, some of the grey bits camouflaged and the posh frock on, I was in high spirits and looking forward to the centenary dinner.

The foyer of the Amatola Hotel was crowded. I had previously arranged to meet a trio of old classmates. I would have known Liz, Doreen and Esmee anywhere and, bless them, they said the same about me. Maybe a little bit more mature with the confidence of successful careers behind them, but they were really still the same girls I had giggled with all these years ago, every time Bertie Grant, our Latin master, nearly set fire to his trousers standing too near the coal burning stove.

I looked around and studied the crowd making their way into the dining room. Could that be Les? Could I approach that woman in the blue dress and say, "Hi, Anita!" and surely that was Johnny, the handsome young boy I had fancied for at least a month in 1954.

The Amatola Hotel did us proud. The meal was delicious and the service was excellent. The noise of chatter and laughter was deafening. The evening was going to be a great success.

There were a few special highlights in the evening for me. Firstly, I instantly recognised Miss Edwards, my old Maths teacher, except 'old' is definitely not the adjective to use for Teddy, who looked far too youthful to have taught me differential calculus forty years ago. I was delighted to talk to her and tell her I had been following in her footsteps for thirty-four years.

I have been exiled in Montrose for most of my married life, and when Aberdeen Academy became Hazlehead Academy, I lost touch and lost interest in my old school. However, I was impressed and moved by the speech of Brian Wood, the present Rector. I, too, had noticed the absence of almost a whole generation of former pupils who had missed out on that fine feeling of pride in the traditions of one's old school.

For me, of course, the real highlight of the evening was Mr Goldie's speech. As he spoke, I could almost smell the old classroom with the coal burning stove, and the freshness of the frosty Saturday mornings when I pounded up the left wing of the hockey pitches at Harlaw.

I remembered the cold fear when Jock Robertson, Mr Goldie's predecessor, entered the classroom with the report cards. And I remembered the pride I felt when I sang in the school Christmas concerts. I never sing "O Come All Ye Faithful" without recalling that in my schooldays, I sang it in Latin, "Adeste Fideles, Laete Triumphantes."

I dearly wanted to speak to Mr Goldie after the dinner, but even now, after all these years, I still felt some trepidation. I wanted to tell him something. Almost forty years ago exactly, he summoned the parents of a certain rebellious teenager and advised them not to allow her to leave school at fifteen. That one concerned act of yours shaped my happy life and career. Thank you, Mr Goldie, and God bless you.

The evening culminated in the singing of the school song. Led by the sweet voice of Laura Brand, we sang with gusto and feeling, "Ad Altiora Tendo," (I am reaching for higher things.) The song has inspired thousands of young Aberdonians for many decades.

On behalf of all those former pupils at the dinner and all the others in far flung parts of the world who couldn't be there, thank you, School, congratulations on your centenary, and here's to the next hundred.

Three

Nature Articles

Table Talk

(Published in the "Scottish Home and Country Magazine October 1996)

My husband has built a chain of luxury restaurants in the north east of Scotland. All of them are in the most select areas and offer haute cuisine at its best to some of the pickiest customers in the land. But my darling partner is not one of Scotland's richest tycoons. In fact he has given all of his restaurants to family and friends except for the original one, which we manage personally.

We have never been accused of inept, lazy or rude service and we have never needed to advertise. The word is passed by tweet of beak.

Our magnificent eating place with empty flat above available for rent, and nearby bath house, is situated just a few feet away from our sun lounge window. It stands six feet off the ground and has a modern slatted roof to protect our little birds from the rain. The main floor has drainage and a raised edge to prevent some of our more enthusiastic eaters spilling their dinner on to the flowers below.

We keep a fairly constant menu (our customers demand it) but we are always willing to do a special "dish of the day" and watch the response. Yesterday "parfait of porridge," salt forgotten...er... *omitted* for healthy eating, was popular only with the starlings, the lager-louts of the bird world, so this will not be repeated. However my "raisin rockies," (a disastrous version of Delia Smith's idiot proof muffin recipe,) and "noisettes of traditional farmhouse cheese," (half price at the supermarket and as tasty as chopped tennis balls,) disappeared in minutes when the sparrows were down.

The sparrows are our bar lunch customers. They arrive in large noisy groups, taste everything on the menu with an exceeding lack of good manners and leave the table in a disgraceful mess. Then they fly over for a quick splash in our mixed bathing facility. With the bath near emptied, they then flail about in the dry soil around the roses, which is perhaps the spuggy equivalent of a dust with talcum powder.

Our favourite customers are the blue tits, the acrobats of the garden. They get through pounds of peanuts, but their special favourite is "swinging coconut picked from waving palms in a tropical dawn," and they feed upside down for minutes at a time. Their larger relation, the great tit, with its broad black band down the centre of its front, likes coconut too, but if they are on the menu, he selects our specially prepared ornitho-kebabs with raisins, bacon, cake and nuts, skewered on to a length of wire and hung from the edge of the table. Our kebabs are also popular with our handsome chaffinch with his pink breast and bluish cap. The female is much duller, although both have two white bands on each wing. She always chooses exactly the same food as her mate.

The blackbird is a real character. One minute he is singing like Placido Domingo, the next he has us rushing inside to answer a silent phone. He is a connoisseur in apples and is not happy about being offered the last bruised one in the bowl. He demands Galas or Macintosh Reds, freshly chopped and served on a dinner plate.

The brown speckle-breasted thrush is partial to the odd piece of apple, but frankly he is a worm freak and we have never included these in our menu. However if pulling and stretching four inch worms until they are twice the length and swallowing them in one slithery gulp is his idea of a tasty dinner, then that's all right with us...as long as we are not eating spaghetti at the same time...

Our little robin, a solitary soul, loves me more than his fellow birdy beings. Unconcerned that I am washing dishes, he sits on the kitchen window sill and eats his crumbs of "Madeira cake with a hint of lemon," and quite regularly knocks on the glass if he thinks something is wrong with the service. Robbie always bathes alone, usually just before dusk, whistling loudly to let everyone know that he is in the bathroom.

One morning in March, we pulled back the curtains to the most wondrous sight. Seven exotic creatures were sitting on the wall. They had pink crests and red tips on the wing feathers and a quick look in the avian "Who's Who?" confirmed that they were waxwings. They were unimpressed with the menu. "Berries," they twirped, "We only eat berries, aren't there any berries?" Delighted to attract passing trade of this calibre, we rummaged in the freezer for a box of brambles picked around Loch Muick the previous autumn. Alas they did not wait for the defrosting and flew off, complaining angrily that our restaurant did not deserve its five-feather status.

Unfortunately, our premises need rigorous policing. Our clients have often started a skirmish over a peanut but now their lives are in constant danger. Sparkle, whose fur is only partially camouflaged in the white heather, is a persistent, although not very successful, serial killer. Our grandchildren act as bouncers at the weekend. "It's that bad Sparkle again, Grandma!" they cry and they escort him from the garden. He leaves reluctantly with an arrogant swing of his handsome tail and returns five minutes later.

We went off recently and forgot to put up a notice saying "Closed for two weeks due to holidays." We returned to find the restaurant in a sorry state. Every scrap of food had been looted, the bath was in a disgusting mess and the empty coconut shells clattered forlornly in the wind. The cat with no-one to murder was serenely asleep on the roof of the shed. Before unpacking, or even putting on the kettle, we quickly tidied and restocked.

Miraculously, somewhere in the trees, birdy binoculars were focused on the garden. The news spread. "Tell everyone, that's them home again. What does she look like in these shorts! Yes, they're opening up again! Grub's up, lads!"

Golfing in the sun was fine but we really had missed our wee birds. And, after all, we do have a business to run.

Nuts to Sammy

(This article was published in the Scottish Home and Country March 1998)

The Edinburgh branch of our family-owned chain of birdy restaurants has been invaded by a convicted terrorist and Bruce and Ann, my son and daughter-in-law, are delighted.

The bird table, which caters for the dietary requirements of every species of garden bird is situated at the bottom of the garden near a little copse of trees. From there, Sammy, a large grey squirrel, makes regular forays over and down the fence headfirst, up the pole and onto the feeding platform. He steals everything that Ann provides for the birds, including peanuts, grain and seeds, chopped apples and pears and fat-balls. Sometimes he does his circus act and swings upside down for minutes at a time, munching on the coconut, which the blue tit considers to be his own personal property.

Sammy is particularly partial to a pea pod or a plum, the Marks and Spencer's bread with the sunflower seeds on top, and although Ann watches his cholesterol intake, he occasionally gets one fat chip.

Visitors to the new house warn Ann and Bruce that their uninvited guest will be nothing but trouble. The grey squirrel was the unwelcome North American immigrant who was first introduced into Britain over a hundred years ago. Initially, they were exhibited in the London Zoo, then in the splendid gardens of the rich and famous. Since then, they have been steadily advancing over the country. My husband (who has never owned a gun!) threatens to shoot poor Sammy and make him into a squirrel pie and a Davy Crocket hat.

But Ann and Bruce are enchanted by him and spend many hours just admiring his antics. Sammy is indeed the most beautiful creature. With the confidence of one who knows he is exquisite, he sits on the fence allowing Ann to photograph him from all angles, showing off his magnificent grey-brown tail, his silky white chest and his alert little face with dark eyes set at the sides of his head for good all round vision.

However, despite their beauty, grey squirrels have had a very bad press. It has even been said that they are vermin. Isn't it a shame that any species which is very successful is labelled this way? If the grey is unpopular, then his cousin, the smaller, daintier red, is the darling of the family, the Squirrel Nutkin of the Beatrix Potter books, the cuddly toy, the attractive little animal in a wintry scene on a Christmas card.

The grey squirrel is said to be the sworn enemy of the red and responsible for the rapid decline in their numbers. This suggests that there is full-scale warfare going on in the woods. But squirrels are peaceable animals. There is no biting with razor sharp teeth, no fisticuffs with delicate front paws and red and grey fur flying everywhere.

In fact Sammy is a big softie. A glimpse of the cat at the window next door and he disappears over the fence like snow off the Calton Hill in August. He even has a healthy respect for the sparrows who fly down to the bird table for their bar lunch. They tell him politely to shove off and he retreats to the fence where he sits and chatters to himself until the birds are finished. Sometimes, if it is cold and he is having to wait too long, he wraps his tail round his neck like a furry scarf.

Contrary to popular belief, squirrels do not hibernate in winter. Nor does Sammy appear to use the bird restaurant as a "take-away." However, who knows, somewhere behind the fence, there may be a huge cache of nutty treats, stored for a "rainy day."

The red squirrel is a shy animal who prefers to eat his unpalatable diet of seed cones in deep undisturbed coniferous forests. In many parts of Britain, but thankfully not in Scotland, the pine forests have been cut down and the native animal has been unable to adapt to an alternative habitat.

Sammy and his friends, on the other hand, are not too concerned about the disappearance of the coniferous forests. He is not averse to stealing a pine cone from under the red squirrel's nose, but he really prefers to live in tall broad leafed trees such as the sycamore, oak and beech. He has proved that he can easily survive in habitats created for humans.

The tall trees at the foot of the garden in Torphin Bank along with the bird table for extra treats are just what Sammy needs to be a happy healthy squirrel.

If he misbehaves, (and the family warn that this may happen) some squirrel-proofing measures will be taken and Sammy might just need to find that buried store of goodies behind the fence. But provided he keeps his paws off the newly planted bulbs, and doesn't bring round too many of his pals, the little grey rascal will be as welcome as the birds in the garden at Torphin Bank.

The Life and Times of a Basin Bird

(This article won the Marty Duncan trophy for the best amusing article at the SAW Conference in March, 1999.)

My name is Malcolm and I'm a totally gorgeous mallard duck. My head is shiny green, which contrasts beautifully with my yellow beak. My breast is a splendid brownish purple colour set off by a snowy white collar; my speculum, the magnificent flash in my tail feathers, is royal blue fringed with white and my legs and feet are dazzling orange.

So you'd think with my breathtaking beauty, the bird watchers up at the Montrose Wildlife Centre would find it hard to keep their binoculars and cameras off me. But when I swim with my pals in front of the viewing windows, they say, "Oh, there's nothing very interesting out there in the water today," and they point their binoculars skywards to a buzzard looking for his mid-morning snack. It's hurtful but I don't get too upset. They say the same about the eiders, the moorhens and the oystercatchers.

Sometimes I envy my cousin Donald, who flew away to have a quiet life on a village pond. He is always the centre of attention... but mostly from obnoxious two-year olds who shout "Duckies! Quack! Quack!" and hurl stale buns at his head. At least I know that however peckish I get, my next lunch is never more than six hours away, when the tide goes out.

I live on Montrose Basin, which is a 2000-acre enclosed estuary. Twice a day it is filled and emptied by the tide, and seawater mixes with the fresh water of the river South Esk. When the tide flows out, it leaves a wonderful feast of worms and molluscs. But time and tide wait for no ducks and I have to hurry on to the mud to get the choicest morsels. I'm not a fussy eater. I like most things including the odd insect. I sometimes take a little paddle along to the west end of the Basin for a beakful or two of waste grain. The Ranger scatters this twice a day in an attempt to keep the swan population off the fields. Fat chance! But oh, I never get tired of a tasty lugworm or a juicy shrimp fresh out of the mud. I share this daily harvest with 20,000 other birds and we all get on together rather well. Some, like the widgeon, shovelers, teal and scaup, only come for the winter, but like us, the eiders, moorhens and a few red breasted mergansers stay the whole year round. We're fairly friendly with the waders too. The knot and dunlin, curlews and godwits, the oystercatchers, redshanks and snipe all like the same food as I do. But the Basin is virtually untouched by industrial pollution and there is enough food for us all.

In May, the swallows, warblers and martins arrive from Africa. They fly high in the early summer skies and sing for sheer joy all day long. The sun shines and my partner Marilla and I rear our new family. I'm one very happy little duck.

But in the autumn the wild geese come. They don't arrive all at once though. The first pink-footed geese fly in from Iceland and Greenland at the end of September, the numbers increase rapidly in October, and by November 33,000 have decided to take their winter holidays in Montrose. Now I haven't just made up this number. There are volunteers up at the Wildlife Centre, who have nothing better to do than count them. It beats me how they do it. It takes all my mathematical skills to count my own ducklings. (Eight last year, and all doing well, thank you.)

What really gets up my beak is that they are supposed to be rare...in spite of their throngs. Montrose Basin, I'm told, is an internationally important place for pink-footed geese. Well, I'd really be interested to know what's so special about them. They are fat and ugly. In contrast to my magnificent colours their plumage is mousy brown, they walk with their toes turned in and their feet and legs are the colour of cheap rubber gloves. But bird watchers come from all over the country and even from abroad *just* to see them. Well-known ornithologists make special visits to study them. Famous artists paint them and poets are inspired to write their very best lines. And my drop-down-in-a-faint gorgeousness goes quite unnoticed.

I always know by instinct when it's first light, but no one could sleep late when the pink-foots are here. The skies above Montrose are filled with their clamour as they fly off to spend the day pillaging and foraging in the surrounding farmlands. Do they think the winter wheat was planted just for them?

I have to admit that their mass flights silhouetted against a pink dawn sky are quite impressive. But nothing to get out of bed for! Would you believe it, the local bird-watchers organise goose breakfasts? No, they don't eat the geese, more's the pity. They meet at 6.30 am and huddle together in the cold with their binoculars and telescopes focused on every skein. They count them and get all excited when they spot an interloper. It isn't always the case of birds of a feather flocking together. Sometimes barnacle geese, Canada geese and greylag go along for the ride. Afterwards, over bacon butties and coffee back in the warmth of the Wildlife Centre, some one claims to have seen an immature female snow goose... and they get excited all over again.

The days are growing longer and warmer and at last the geese are making tracks for their breeding grounds in the Arctic. The morning and evening skies over Montrose are now strangely quiet. It's spring and Marilla has found a nice wee spot for our nest this year. It's right in front of the viewing gallery at the Centre.

That should attract some attention.

The Importance of Being Fergus

My name is Fergus and I'm a young wild pheasant. It's almost impossible to describe how handsome I am, but just look at my picture and try not to faint. When the sun shines, my fiery coppery feathers gleam like burnished gold and the contrast between my metallic green neck and scarlet wattle is simply stunning.

I am king of Edzell golf course and workmen tend my mature trees, lush fairways and manicured greens all year round.

For a few weeks in late spring I lived with my five wives but every one of them was so drab and uninteresting, I don't know why I bothered. Long before my chicks were hatched, I was off. Some birds, I know, are involved in the rearing of their young, but I'm a macho pheasant. This modern sharing, caring daddy stuff is not in my nature.

Mind you, my wives were not much better. Without exception they were terrible mothers, especially in bad weather. They sat on their nests long enough for one or two chicks to hatch and then got bored looking out at the rain. So off they went, without as much as a backward maternal glance, abandoning the rest of the chicks to the foxes and crows. They are a disgrace to the species! Just as well there's a gamekeeper in the district who looks after things, incubating eggs and hand rearing the young poults or we would be heading for glorious extinction like the long dead dodo. This kind man keeps the pheasants as pets and I'm descended from one who went walkabout two seasons ago.

Just before my dalliance with the hens I wasn't myself at all. For a couple of weeks I felt so territorial and bad tempered that I often kicked the living daylights out of some of my best pals...and, would you believe it, the rows were all over these unattractive females who just stood around quite unconcerned. However, it must have been something I ate, because I'm fine now. In fact I'm back to my usual happy self and friendly with all the lads again. Why I, Fergus the Gorgeous, was the slightest bit interested in these silly hens, I can't imagine. Frankly, I now prefer to look at the lady golfers, especially in the summer when they wear brightly coloured shorts and tops. (The male of the human species is drab and uninteresting all year round.)

I spend all my life enjoying myself. I eat a wide range of food and I don't have to go far to get it. My favourite is the wheat in a nearby field. But everybody adores me so I visit a lot, especially in the winter. I simply strut into the local gardens and somebody shouts, "It's Fergus!" and I'm offered all sorts of tasty things. To be honest, I'm rather fat. Getting airborne to clear the fence between the field and the golf course is becoming rather a challenge.

Sometimes I wander about on the roads just outside the course. I love to play 'chicken,' especially on blind corners. It's fun making cars screech to a halt as I dart from side to side. I am glad I can still run fast, as the other day, that careless postman in the red van didn't even stop. Alas, a few of my dear departed chums were not as young and agile as I am. I saw poor old Ferdinand lying at the side of the road....well, I don't need to draw you a picture, do I?

The ladies going down to the practise range always acknowledge that I am king of the road. They stop their cars and simply sit back and admire me. They say how lovely I am,...well, I know that!...but with bread sauce and game chips?...what *are* they talking about?

I have my greatest fun on the golf course, especially on ladies' day. I used to hurry over the fairway, scared that I might be knocked senseless by a flying golf ball, but now, I just stroll leisurely across and make them wait.

Sometimes I stand near the tee. I don't move until the first lady prepares to play her shot. I watch as she goes through her routine (head still, eye on the ball, slowly back.) Then as she brings the club forward, I let rip with my very loudest 'korok-kok' and I beat my wings furiously. I have to laugh. She either misses the ball completely or slices it deep into the woods. Although I don't dare repeat this for her playing partners, they always hit rather nervous shots and set off down the fairway gibbering about deep freezers and hot ovens.

Freddie is the tough old bird who perches on the seat at the short fourteenth hole and takes bets on how many balls will land in the bunkers. He says that I am as naïve as a turkey writing his Christmas card list, and that life will not always be such fun. Like me, he hops over to the fields for his dinner, but he never stays long. He's got a great sense of drama, has Fred, and is forever making apocalyptic utterances. He glances over at the farming lands and whispers chillingly about the killing fields where, from October to February, men with guns and dogs will shoot for sport and take no prisoners. He warns that sometimes they even have a 'cock-shoot' when wily old campaigners like himself, and even regal young birds like me are assassinated, sparing the stupid hens for breeding.

His advice is 'Walk, don't fly,' because they shoot at anything above six feet.

But this makes no sense at all. As I see it, my purpose in life, along with the deer, red squirrels, hares and the rest of a wonderful wealth of wildlife, is to make the golf course even more attractive to members and visitors.

However, to be on the safe side, I'm not moving far from the fairway.

I, Fergus, will always be safe with the ladies.

Four

Teaching Days

Exam Fever

(Published in the P&J May 2006)

A large section of the teenage population will voluntarily ground themselves this month because all over the UK exam fever is raging.

The 'big ones,' the Standard Grade and Higher exams in Scotland and the GCSE's and A levels elsewhere, start for most candidates in May, kicking off with English followed closely by Maths. The rest drag on through the entire month and for schools south of the border, well into June.

By now, the reluctant examinees are reconciled to the fact that Mum is unlikely to win the lottery, thus allowing them to skip all exams and live a life of idleness for ever. Nor, unfortunately, is there to be an examination invigilators' strike. Serious study is now, therefore, a matter of some urgency.

For most youngsters this is the first real stress in their lives and you can be sure that they won't suffer alone. The entire house has to walk on egg shells. While the books are out, there has to be a monastic silence. No vacuuming, no gossipy cups of tea with the next door neighbour in the kitchen, no Classic FM.

Any extraneous noise, like the sun passing behind a cloud, can cause a minor nervous breakdown. But, as everyone knows, *Arctic Monkeys* blasting through the headphones of the i-Pod is an important aid to concentration.

A teenager without a social life is like a golden eagle without his tail feathers. Trapped in a bedroom with a mountain of notes on *Macbeth*, trigonometry and French irregular verbs, each day is so boring that it is not even worthwhile getting dressed. On non exam days, the great unwashed will wander about in jammies, hair uncombed and wild looking, occasionally muttering nonsense like "all sine tan cos" or "Unsex me here. And fill me from the crown to the toe top full of direst cruelty!" to no-one in particular. But the dog flees for his life.

Study brings on ravenous hunger. So every hour on the hour, coffee is made and four more chocolate digestives disappear from the biscuit tin.

The phone will be red hot, to confirm that pals are suffering likewise and haven't escaped to the sports centre.

But on exam days there will be a transformation. Most schools insist on normal uniform but the teachers never go near the examination hall to check up. The correct gear is important for confidence and comfort. For both sexes the top three buttons of the shirt must be open...exam halls are notoriously stifling as the early summer sun beats in on the poor unfortunates at their desks. The knot of the school tie must be at waist level as any higher up would cut off the blood supply to the brain. And then there are the essential lucky mascots. Miniature teddy bears exchanged on Valentine Day are favoured by everyone.

After the ordeal is over, the victim will arrive home, either disappointed and white-faced with exhaustion or with a "No sweat, it was a dawdle," nonchalance. Neither reaction is the slightest indication of pass or fail. All Mum needs to do at this stage is to appear cool and casual and ready to cook the favourite supper.

Exam fever is like spring fever. It only lasts for a few weeks. There may be a little more anxiety when the results arrive in that distinctive brown envelope three months later.

But in the teenage timescale, that is light years away.

DMs For Dancing

(This article was published in the P&J on 20 December, 1994)

Christmas Dance fever is at its height in school this week. Kilts have been hired, jeans washed and dresses bought. But first partners have to be found as a matter of urgency.

Early teenage romances are conducted by a complicated system of furtive whisperings and note passing as the matchmakers and appointed go-betweens get to work. Then negotiations duly completed, the affair is out in the open and the happy couple sit beside each other in class, and the schoolwork continues without further disruption.

It doesn't always go so well, though. Overheard in the corridor: "You must be joking! I think he's had a charisma bypass. And look at his ears!"

The "with it" party gear for girls this Christmas is a dress in any colour as long as it's black. If it is not black, it must have been purchased in Outer Mongolia or, heaven forbid, it is last year's dress.

The most popular design looks like a thin silk underslip, so for the sake of decency, the girls need to wear a white T-shirt underneath. Matching white knee socks and heavy black Doctor Marten boots complete the outfit. Some of the girls have bought shiny lighter weight boots. Who would have thought it? DMs for dancing!

We may have a wee smile at all this sartorial eccentricity, but were we any more elegant forty years ago?

I remember my first school Christmas Dance. My mother always shopped at the Co-op, (mindful of her dividend, 2/6 in the £) and joy of joys, they stocked the "in gear" for Christmas 1954, the reversible fully circular taffeta skirt, black on one side and red on the other. We all wore them, cinched in at the waist with a wide elastic belt and mounted on so many petticoats that we took up two seats on the bus. What I wore on my top half, I have conveniently erased from my memory. On very rare occasions, and only when I'm dancing the *Dashing White Sergeant*, I have a nightmarish picture of wisps of cotton wool appearing at the neck of some low cut garment, dislodged from the 32 AA cup bra I had so carefully padded. White ankle socks, flattie shoes and a Fair Isle cardigan knitted by my granny, completed the picture of high fashion. Those of us who were truly sophisticated wore bright red lipstick and huge white pan-drop earrings with powerful clips that gripped your earlobes like some medieval torture.

Our music and fashion were imported from the States. Our fantasy was to look like the fresh faced Doris Day or the dainty Debbie Reynolds.

It took the greatest courage to ask Raymond, the boy I loved for most of my early teenage years, to the school dance. Apart from my excessive shyness, I had a dad who killed all my youthful yearnings stone dead. The Co-op milk horse, a creature of habit, used to deposit a large steaming heap on the street near Raymond's house and my dad used to go and shuffle it up. Dad's roses flourished but although Raymond did come to the dance with me, my love was unrequited.

We all thought we looked great in our 1954 Christmas party outfits, but no one ever confirmed it. At the pictures we watched the American "mom" gaze lovingly at her daughter descending the wide staircase into the open-plan lounge with its enormous Christmas tree. Young Miss America was ready to go off to her first school prom with a handsome, crew cut beau. "Oh honey, you look gorgeous," Mom would whisper with a tear in her eye, "I am so proud of you!" With a toss of her long blonde hair and a flash of her perfect white teeth, this human Barbie doll would stride out confidently to the waiting car.

My mum would look me up and down and say, "Hm, you have been squeezing that spot on your chin again! And wear your wellies. It's pouring rain!"

Teenagers still seek adult approval. Few of them have more than the thinnest veneer of confidence. So this week at the Christmas Dance, I'll tell them truthfully that I think they look great. Maybe I'll even feel a wee bit envious of these cute young visions in their black and white uniforms, the DMs stomping rhythmically to the beat of "Wet, Wet, Wet," the look of new love on their fresh young faces.

They might ask me to join them for the *Dashing White Sergeant.*

I just hope nobody steps on my toes.

Ode To Pythagoras
(And All Who Have Known Him)

(This article was published in the P&J in October 1995 and is now the basis for Liz's effort at a book called *A Slice of Pi*)

I found an old book tucked away in a corner of the maths store. In the preface to *Real Life Arithmetic for Girls,* published in 1937, the author writes, "The average girl will not be much interested in mathematics. It is advisable, however, that she is able to add together sums of money so that she can check the bill in a teashop and present accurate household accounts to her husband."

In the same book, the girl is encouraged to use a ruler accurately by making a paper pattern for a pair of knickers. The instructions read, "Measure the full height of the person for whom the garment is intended. The length of the knickers will be 7/16 of this height in a normal person. The width will be 1⅜ times the length." Hopefully, wartime shortages would have ensured that these voluminous mega-bloomers never got beyond the paper pattern stage. On the other hand, they might have made pretty effective parachutes.

There is nothing so mysterious as mathematics to those who have never learned any. This mystery stretches back to the ancient Greeks and it is only in the second part of the 20th century that every child, irrespective of ability, learns several branches of mathematics, even if only at foundation level.

Before this, pupils considered to be not mathematically inclined, learned only a limited form of arithmetic. In this category came most girls. In our less sexist, more enlightened times, maths is no longer an esoteric subject studied only by a select few and regarded by the rest as incomprehensible mumbo-jumbo. Good, modern teachers understand that maths ability is not a divine gift, but one which will develop as a result of the learning process.

The march of mathematical knowledge has been guided by the 'stars,' those individuals of great genius from the days of the ancient Greeks to the computer experts of today.

The first mathematical sage we know anything about is Pythagoras, who lived from 580 to 500 BC. On the Greek island of Samos, he set up a secret society devoted to exploring the mysteries of number.

The society allowed women on an equal basis which was very unusual in these days. Indeed, Theano, his wife, was no mean mathematician herself, but she never got into the news like her husband.

Pythagoras is credited with the famous theorem but almost certainly it was known in Egypt, from pyramid building. The story goes that Pythagoras was sitting outside on his patio which was laid out in fine marble slabs of different shapes. Suddenly he had a mathematical thought, or theorem as he called it. "I wonder if that marble square laid along the longest side of that right-angled triangle equals the sum of the squares laid along the two shorter sides." He called the longest side the "hypotenuse" just to make it more mysterious.

Well, he was right, it did and he proved it. Now, over 2500 years later, Class 2 youngsters do interesting little problems about ladders leaning against walls and taking short cuts diagonally across a rectangular field with a bull in it.

Pythagoras was one of these super-intelligent geniuses who ended up being two degrees short of a right angle.

He firmly believed that God made the universe from whole numbers so, when one of the members of his hippy mathematical commune, Hippasus, kept ranting on about numbers he had discovered which couldn't be calculated exactly, like $\sqrt{2}$, they drowned him for not keeping his mouth shut.

Numbers which cannot be calculated exactly are called irrational numbers and my pupils are quite familiar with them. When we are studying the circle, the class and I go out to the social area (formerly called the playground) and draw large chalk circles, measure the diameter and circumference by walking toe to heel across and around and so calculate π (pi.) For school calculations, π = 3.14, but my pupils know that the figures go on for ever. We have a frieze round the classroom walls 3.141592654….which could be extended down the corridor and out the door and on and on….

Over the centuries, several mathematicians have devoted their lives to calculating π to 30, 50, and more decimal places and now by modern computer methods, the king of the irrational numbers has been calculated to millions of places, and the digits never appear in a repeated pattern.

Along came Euclid, 250 years after Pythagoras. We don't know much about him. He never went to the local tavern with his chums in Alexandria. He was too busy writing "Elements" a great work about geometry in thirteen volumes, and for the next 2500 years, that's the geometry school children had to learn. Mercifully, the children of today are spared these mysterious propositions and axioms which bedevilled the scholars of yesteryear, myself included.

Nor is much known about the life of Al Khwarizmi, an Arabian mathematician who lived in the 8th century. His book on algebra (al-jabr means the science of equations) gave a name to this branch of maths.

Algebra is like arithmetic, but uses letters and symbols to represent numbers and form equations to solve problems. Children love algebra, agreeing with me that there is nothing better for the soul than solving a tricky little equation.

By Class 3, most of my pupils are ready and able to start trigonometry, a cocktail of algebra and geometry, useful whenever lengths and angles of a triangle have to be calculated.

Aryabhata, a 6th century teacher of mathematics, laid down a basis for trigonometry by developing a table of 'sines.' From day one, children shorten the word to 'trig' and take to the subject as if the ratios sine, cosine and tangent (sin, cos, tan) had been in their vocabulary from the beginning.

When I teach them about number patterns, my pupils like to hear the story of Karl Friedrich Gauss, the great 19th century mathematician and astronomer. When he was a young schoolboy, his teacher, exhausted like any other teacher on a Friday afternoon, thought he would keep the class quietly occupied for some time by asking them to add up the numbers from 1 to 100. Well, young Gauss came up with the answer in seconds. In case you haven't worked it out yet, the answer is 5050. Our little brain of Germany had invented the formula N multiplied by N + 1, divided by 2. (100 x 101 ÷2 = 5050)

In Class 5, my Higher pupils start calculus, invented simultaneously by Isaac Newton in England and Gottfried Wilhelm Leibniz in Germany, in the early 18th century.

There is a certain snobbery about studying calculus. If you reach this stage, you are one of the elite. A non-mathematician, opening a book on calculus will see inscrutable, secret stuff with wonderfully weird notations and symbols. But within days, Class 5 took to it like a dot to a decimal.

To be famous in Edinburgh, your deeds and eccentricities have to be on a large scale and that was true of John Napier. He was a magician and the imaginative seer of present day submarines. He dabbled in the black arts but was also a frenzied anti-papist, living at the same time as Mary Queen of Scots, the Roman Catholic queen who got her head chopped off.

Napier was also a brilliant mathematician and his work on logarithms was immediately welcomed by contemporary scientists and engineers. Until calculators made them unnecessary, most 14-year-olds were familiar, but not in love, with logs. Now the theory of logarithms comes near the end of the break-neck Higher course. By this time, my poor pupils have lapsed into terminal brain shut down and they groan their way through log functions.

Then we approach modern times. John Babbage, in the mid 19th century, was a man way ahead of his time. He invented a giant sized mechanical computer, but because of money shortage it was never completed, until a few years ago. The modern engineers who built it found that Babbage's plans were perfect and the machine functioned as he had intended.

My boys and girls often ask about these star mathematicians. Were they really very clever? I try to tell them that we are where we are now, intellectually speaking, because they were there then. We live on the mental capital accumulated by these brilliant people and will be eternally grateful to Pythagoras and his successors.

Certainly I have enjoyed teaching mathematics for more than thirty years. It is marvellous that there is so much yet to be discovered and, hopefully a whole new galaxy of mathematical stars will light the way.

School's Out For Ever

(Published in the Press & Journal 28 June 1995. This short article
prompted many readers to write in with their best wishes)

Today is my last day. Goodbye school. The Queen Bee of Room
12A has taught her last lesson, corrected the very last jotter.
My thirty-six year obsession for arriving at school at 8.30 am is
now cured.

It was time to retire. The signs were all there, the desire to have
a wee sleep at lunch time, the tendency to file the daily contents of
my pigeon hole in the staff room under B for bin. And for someone
for whom high technology meant operating a pencil sharpener and
refilling the stapler, these new machines edging their way into my
classroom with more gigabytes than I have teeth were becoming a
threat.

I have thrown out all my school clothes, the navy skirts, the
tailored blouses, the chunky hand-knitted jumpers for when the
classroom temperature was sub-zero. So now I have the wardrobe
of a plucked chicken. But tomorrow I will be off to the big city
for gear more suited to the nouveau retired, clothes for walking,
dancing, golf and popping up to the Arctic Circle on a P&J mini-
break.

But I cannot throw away my memories so carelessly. I haven't
only been teaching percentages, pie charts and Pythagoras for all
these years, I have been teaching children. So every day of these
thirty-six years has been a kaleidoscope of colourful events, ever
different, often frustrating but never boring.

I never chased the well-paid jobs outside the classroom. George
Bernard Shaw said, "He who can, does. He who cannot, teaches."

Maybe so, but those who can teach well, should teach and leave the others to write the jargon, regurgitate old pedagogical philosophies and wear posh suits upon which chalk dust would not dare to settle.

My priority has always been the youngsters in my classroom, because it is from them that I have derived the fun and the satisfaction from my profession.

I have limped home at 4pm on Fridays looking like Methuselah but at least the kids have kept me young at heart. How many other grannies can converse knowledgeably about the pop charts and teenage fashion?

However, I did cheat last week. Kirsty in 4G asked me if I liked *Unchained Melody*. I burst into song (badly) "Oh my love my darling one, I hunger for your touch, a long lonely time. Time goes by so slowly and dum dum dum de dum…" She was mightily impressed, and I nearly confessed that I was about her age when I smooched around the dance floor to that same hit song away back in the 1950s. Ah me, how the years have flown by.

I would like to think that I have given some of my pupils a wee helping hand along the way. For some, an extra lunchtime lesson to ensure they got that vital Higher for university, for others a few words to boost a confidence with an eggshell fragility, for others the ability to make sense of their income tax in later life. In return they have given me so much more.

So this is my last day. I want to go but it is hard to leave.

Tomorrow and all the other days will be like one long sunny Saturday. But just for today, leave me with my retirement cards and my Kleenex.

Memories of 35 years at the Chalk Face

(This article won the John Severn trophy for the best article at the SAW Conference in March 2007 I was naughty and used some anecdotes from a previous article.)

Ten years ago, I said goodbye to school. The Queen Bee of Room 12A had taught her last lesson and corrected the very last jotter. My thirty-five year obsession for arriving at school at 8.30 am was over.

It was time to retire. The signs were all there, the desire to have a little nap at lunch time and the irritation at what seemed to be unnecessary and meaningless paperwork. And, although in my retired years I have become an ardent technophile with a study that looks like the operations room at NASA Space Station, I was well aware then that my pupils knew more about computers than I did.

I threw out all my school clothes, the navy skirts, the tailored blouses, the chunky hand knitted jumpers for when the heating had broken down and the classroom temperature was sub zero. This left the wardrobe of a plucked turkey, but the following day I was off to the city for gear more suited to the nouveau retired, clothes for walking, dancing, golf and frequent holidays in sunny climes.

But I couldn't throw away my memories so carelessly. For all those years I didn't only teach every topic of mathematics from decimals to differential equations, I was teaching children. So every day of these thirty-five years was a kaleidoscope of colourful events, ever different, often frustrating, increasingly exhausting, but never boring.

I remember my first day as a very young teacher in August 1960.

After the morning break, I was making my way along a crowded corridor to my classroom. An elderly man grabbed my shoulder and pulled me to the side. "Girl!" he shouted. "How many times do you need to be told? Keep to the left!" After a bad start, the Head of the Physics department and I became good friends and he danced at my wedding.

The first few years were difficult. At five feet one inch and weighing seven stone I looked too young to be a teacher but I was enthusiastic about my subject and I soon established a rapport with my pupils. Eventually I wouldn't have done any other job in the world, even at twice the salary.

In 1971, Princess Margaret opened our new school. In Scotland the mini skirt was still fashionable and mine, bought especially for the occasion, was all of eighteen inches. However, the Princess was wearing the new midi length, a beautiful suit in the palest silver grey with the skirt to mid calf. With this she wore a magnificent hat and grey boots with silver heels. She looked absolutely stunning and we were all entranced by her beauty. My skirts from then on were of a length more appropriate for my profession.

To be a good teacher, you need all sorts of skills; those of a psychologist, nurse, mother, senior member of the United Nations peacekeeping force and on school trips, the ability to go without sleep for days. Once on a skiing holiday in Austria, we shared our hotel with a school party from Italy; the handsome olive skinned heartthrobs from Sorrento were just too much of a temptation for my girls so I had to do a very strict night watch and be on duty throughout the day also. The ironic thing was that people used to comment on the 'free' holidays that teachers got. On another trip, I stayed behind in France whilst one of my pupils was treated in hospital for a dog bite and on one occasion our bus was held up at Calais for eighteen hours because of a French lorry drivers' strike. Dealing with sleeping arrangements, meals, toilets and communications with home long before the invention of mobile phones was the stuff of nightmares. Although our kids got to miss a day at school when we eventually got home, the staff had to report for duty the following morning.

During my career, I have cured hiccups, dealt with nosebleeds, asthmatic attacks, epileptic fits, broken bones (and hearts) and examination panic. I have even saved a life. Twenty years ago, I was invigilating in the examination hall when a disturbance at the back alerted me that something was wrong. A girl was choking and to my horror, her lips turned blue and she slumped unconscious to the floor. I stuck my fingers down her throat and pulled hard. Out came a broken orthodontic brace along with a huge chunk of strictly forbidden pink bubble gum. Luckily Debbie recovered quickly with only a very sore throat due to my rough attempt at first aid. She works at the check-out at Tesco's now and has four beautiful children. I'll bet they aren't allowed to chew gum.

There has also been lots of laughter as I always believed in the old adage, 'All work and no play makes Jack a dull boy.' I also kept a secret file with amusing absence notes. One said, "Please excuse Henrietta-May for being off school last week. She had diahor (crossed out) dyahoria (crossed out) dihhorea (crossed out), upset bowls, yours sincerely, Mrs Stewart." Another one, also from Mrs Stewart, read "Henrietta-May vomited up the High Street at dinner time so I kept her at home in the afternoon."

Over the years, I had many student teachers in my classroom. My girl pupils fell for the young men and I thought that mathematics was the last thing on the minds of my boys when a particularly attractive young female graduate tried to interest the class in the Theorem of Pythagoras. But once I had a mature student of almost my age. She was a very large lady and even by my standards somewhat old fashioned. I was worried that she wouldn't manage to control the class but they were strangely quiet. It emerged later that she was nursing a fledgling sparrow in her bra and the fluttering movements going on in her jumper had the class quite transfixed.

I remember with pride one year when my entire class of sixteen year-olds got A or B passes in their O level exams. I had pupils who have become university professors, doctors, engineers and scientists and others who have followed me into the teaching profession.

Not all of my pupils have been so clever, though, but I was equally proud of a small class who showed off to a school inspector their ability to count money and give change. One boy even told the inspector that if the total at the supermarket was £4.03, it was a good idea to offer three pence along with the note in order to save the change in the till. These children had learning and behavioural difficulties but that day they were stars.

I never chased the well paid jobs outside the classroom. George Bernard Shaw said, "He who can, does. He who cannot, teaches." Maybe so, but those who can teach well, should teach, and leave the others to write the jargon, regurgitate old pedagogical theories and wear smart clothes upon which chalk dust would not dare to settle. My priority was always the youngsters in my classroom, because it was from them that I derived the fun and satisfaction from my profession.

I may have limped home at four o'clock on a Friday looking like Methuselah but at least the kids kept me young at heart. How many other grannies could converse knowledgeably about the pop charts and teenage fashion?

But once, just before I retired, I cheated a little. One of my pupils asked if I liked *Unchained Melody* by the Righteous Brothers. I burst into song (badly) "O my love, my darling, I've hungered for your touch, a long lonely time. Time goes by so slowly and dum dum dum de dum...." She was mightily impressed and I almost confessed that I was about her age when I smooched around the dance floor to Jimmy Young's version of that same lovely song in 1955. Ah me, how the years flew by.

I would like to think that I have given at least some of my pupils a little helping hand along the way. For some, an extra lunchtime lesson to ensure they got that vital entry qualification for university, for others a few words to boost a confidence with an eggshell fragility, for others the ability to make sense of their income tax in later life. In return they have given me so much more.

When it came to the last day, I wanted to leave, but it was so hard to go. I looked forward to a retirement with every day like one long sunny Saturday and so, for the most part, it has been.

But sometimes I like to remember and wish I could do it all over again.

Five

Travel

North to Alaska

The moment we touched down in Anchorage I knew we were ill-equipped to face the Alaskan climate. My husband and I had packed our rucksacks with waterproofs, fleecy jackets and woolly hats and left our summer clothes with our friends in Seattle. But in the second week in June the temperature was in the eighties and the sun was to shine 21 hours out of every 24.

However, we collected our hired car and after a quick visit to Fred Myer's store, we were kitted out for our week in Alaska, with T-shirts, shorts and hiking boots, all for a fraction of the price we would have paid back home.

Alaska is the 49th state and is one fifth of the entire area of the other forty-eight states of the USA, yet its population is only just over half a million, and half of them live in Anchorage. On that hot Saturday, there were few people in the streets or in the stores. A waiter in a restaurant where we had our first taste of fresh Alaskan red salmon, told us that in the summer most people leave the city at the weekend. Owning a bush plane as well as a car is common and gives easy access to the remote and bountiful fishing spots on three thousand rivers and three million lakes.

In spite of, and perhaps because of its burgeoning oil industry, Anchorage is beautiful. A profusion of flower gardens, and hanging baskets brightened public places throughout the downtown area. There were miles of cycle tracks and everywhere seemed clean, fresh and awash with colour.

Anchorage is an excellent base from which to plan excursions and we had things to do and places to see. The manager of the motel said he loved our 'cute' Scottish accents and insisted on helping us revise our plans for the rest of our holiday, dismissing journeys which were too long. It was he who recommended our mini-cruise in the calm and protected waters of Prince William Sound to see twenty-six glaciers, all named after American universities. From Anchorage we drove forty miles to Portage, then took a short but very exciting trip in the double decker Alaskan Express to Whittier through solid rock tunnels, two miles long.

We were lucky. Sometimes Prince William Sound is misty, but on that June morning the sky was brilliant blue and our cruise in the *Klondyke,* the deluxe high speed catamaran, was spectacular. We spent the entire day viewing the glaciers and the wildlife, sometimes from the warm lounge, but mostly out on deck where our fleecy jackets and woolly hats were much appreciated. Bald eagles with a wingspan of seven feet glinted an evil eye at us as they flew over the boat. Little sea otters lying on their backs, opened shellfish with a stone but made a hasty retreat when a beluga whale decided to swim along-side for a mile or two. The captain assured us that its intentions were entirely playful. He also mentioned that, if we fell overboard, we wouldn't survive for more than five seconds. I think he was referring to the temperature of the water.

The glaciers made eerie rumbling noises and we watched from a safe distance as colossal slabs of ice broke from these melting mountains and smashed into the sea to become icebergs. A sort of booming sound rolled across the water and our boat rocked gently.

The current cost of this unique cruise is only $150 (£88) and includes an 'eat as much as you like' salmon lunch and free coffee throughout the trip.

Next day we were off on our journey northwards along Alaska Highway 3, the most beautiful journey we will probably ever experience. The scenery is diverse, untamed and truly breathtaking. As we rounded a corner about 100 miles along the highway we caught our first glimpse of Mount McKinley glistening white in the summer sunshine.

For tourists this 20,320 feet giant is for photographing only.

Climbing 'Denali,' or 'The Great One' as the Alaskan Indians call it, is for international mountaineers who are well aware of their own mortality. On this magnificent peak winds gusting at 150 mph and a -90°F chill factor are not uncommon.

Along the Highway are attractive gift stores and quaint restaurants serving Alaskan size portions. We stopped at 'Big Sue's' for breakfast. She was disappointed that we refused to match the locals and order the 'full stack' of four dinner plate size pancakes with maple syrup and cream. Her wimpy Scottish customers could manage only a 'quarter stack'…..on two plates.

Alaskans find places by mile markers. These are signs with white numbers on a green background seen periodically along the road. The entrance to Denali National Park is at mile 238. This wild and unspoilt wilderness of six million acres is about one third of the size of Scotland and most of it has never been walked on by human beings. For botanists there are hundreds of species of flowering plants, mosses and lichens which have miraculously adapted to the long sub-arctic winters. The area is inhabited by grizzly bears, black bears, wolves, dall sheep, caribou and moose and smaller animals like chipmunks, porcupines and skunks.

Parts of the park are accessible by shuttle buses. Tourists can opt to stay on the small yellow bus, with binoculars at the ready, or get off at any point along the track and spend the day hiking, rejoining the buses later. There are opportunities for climbing and camping but the rules of the park are strict. Feeding the animals is forbidden and campers must store their food in bear-resistant containers. The chipmunks around the Visitor Centre ignore the rules however, and one bold little fellow jumped into my rucksack and made off with a banana.

We spent three days hiking in the park and a surprise meeting with a wild animal was always a possibility. One morning we were walking on a path when suddenly a large, dangerous-looking moose charged out of a willow thicket. We didn't stop to admire her highly photogenic twin calves and did an Olympic record breaking sprint in the opposite direction.

We never saw a skunk but we certainly knew when one had been around. The smell of their defensive spray must be the worst stench in the world. A Ranger told us that if a human is unlucky enough to meet an angry skunk, all clothing would have to be burned as no detergent is capable of washing out the smell.

During our hikes we avoided close encounters of the grizzly kind by wearing 'bear bells' round our wrists and singing Scots songs. If it hears you coming, a grizzly will get out of your way....or so we were told! But if you meet it face to face, you can run for your life or stand absolutely still. The advice is conflicting and futile, as it's unlikely you'll be around to tell the tale. We saw these 800 pound animals and their cubs several times but always through binoculars and from the safety of the yellow bus.

Of all the terrible hardships that plagued the early gold prospectors a hundred years ago, it was the mosquitoes they hated most. Alaskan mozzies are ferocious, but nowadays, locally purchased repellents are very effective. However, the Scottish midgie has a nasty American cousin which the Alaskans call 'no-see-ums.' They are to be found .....correction .....they find *you*, near fresh water, and like the midgie they hunt in packs. I was told, too late, that they hate the smell of Vick, the stuff you rub on your chest, and I was still scratching no-see-um welts two weeks after I was back home.

On our last full day, we climbed aboard the Alaskan Express at the Denali Park station for a look at Fairbanks, 120 miles further north and just 200 miles short of the Arctic Circle. Unfortunately a 'wee look' at Fairbanks just won't do. Faced with too much to see in too short a time, we chose, along with a party of Japanese tourists, to get rich quick at the *El Dorado* gold mine, a few miles north of the city. As we suspected, the grit in our pans glittered in the sunshine but it was pyrites or fool's gold. On the walls of the museum were sepia photographs from a century ago. The exhausted, bedraggled gold stampeders certainly deserved their hard earned bonanza.

And so, after a last salmon bake, it was time to collect our car and return south to Anchorage. With some reluctance we boarded Alaskan Airlines to Seattle, the first leg of our homeward journey.

We had seen only the merest fraction of this land of superlatives, the longest, the highest, the very loveliest. There's a saying, 'Once you've been to Alaska, you never come all the way home.'

It's true. We left our hearts there.

Doing the Strip in Las Vegas

To support its annual invasion of 34 million tourists, Las Vegas has a resident population of 480,000. So, somewhere in the city, there must be normal life going on, with modest housing, schools and somewhere to buy a pint of milk but in the ten mile long mega-bright, mega-extravagant boulevard known as the Strip, no evidence of this exists.

There are hundreds of clubs, concerts and shows you can visit after dusk with prices reasonable to extortionate. The hottest show in town is the long running Celine Dion's *New Day* in the 4,000-seat Colosseum in Caesar's Palace with tickets ranging from $600 to $1,800.

But surprisingly, a wide variety of spectacular entertainment is absolutely free. Every evening in the Rio Hotel, dancers in masks and brilliant costumes, perform in revolving floats hung from the casino ceiling and throw freebies at their audience. I was delighted to catch a necklace strung with tiny dice.

In the atrium of the Bellagio, an army of horticulturists maintain thousands of plants and trees beautifully arranged alongside fountains, bridges and pagodas. The Bellagio also houses a $300 million art collection which costs only $12 to view. And outside, for free, on a quarter mile lake, 1,200 fountains perform a beautiful water ballet in the sky, enhanced by coloured lights and classical music.

Every fifteen minutes after dark at the Mirage Hotel, a volcano erupts with brilliant orange flames. It's as near to seeing a real volcano as you can get without getting lava on your sandals. Also free at the Mirage is the chance to see in an open air habitat designed for their maximum well being, a collection of rare royal white tigers, magnificent creatures with pink paws and ice blue eyes.

At the Forum shopping area of Caesar's Palace, the floor is laid out like the cobbled streets of ancient Rome and above, the vast ceiling is painted with an ever changing sky from the rosy glow of dawn to the night time twinkling stars.

My particular favourite is the five-star Venetian, where the inside is just like the centre of Venice, with replicas of the Doge's Palace and the Campanile. That day, a young couple were being married in a white satin lined gondola on the quarter mile long 'Grand Canal,' whilst all the designer-clad guests clicked expensive cameras at the edge of the water.

It is difficult to describe how huge is huge in Las Vegas. Well, the new five-star Wynn has, on fifty storeys, 2,700 luxury apartments, each one with fast internet access and flat screened televisions in the bathrooms, twenty-two restaurants, most with celebrity chefs, and a casino with facilities for every gambling game including 1,960 slot machines. There is a 2,000 seat circular theatre, an eighteen-hole golf course, two wedding chapels, shopping malls and swimming pools and a man-made mountain with pine trees and fountains. The Wynn is not for casual package holiday tourists in shorts and unlike all the other hotels, very little of it can be viewed from the Strip. With two friends, my husband and I ventured into one of the bars in the hotel lobby. Including the tip, we paid $80 for four beers and had a brief glimpse of how the other half lives.

We spent our four days just wandering in and out of these wonderful adult pleasure palaces trying hard to find superlatives to describe each new experience. But the place which had us both laughing was the Bonanza Store, the world's largest gift shop, where certainly the world's most vulgar souvenirs are for sale. Who would want a pregnant trailer trash action doll or a cushion stuffed with shredded dollar bills? Seeing me stop to giggle at a $39 battery operated, foul mouthed, larger-than-life plastic parrot, an assistant offered free shipping to the UK if I ordered three or more. However, a flashing miniature slot machine does take pride of place on my kitchen window sill.

Las Vegas is the place to have a wacky wedding. Thousands of couples tie the knot there every year and the places chosen for the ceremony range from the floor of the Grand Canyon, a short helicopter ride from Las Vegas, to 'drive-through, don't even bother to get out of your car' quickie weddings at a window of the Little White Chapel. The chapel isn't pretty or romantic, set as it is between porn shops and strip clubs, but it has been the setting for some of the most famous weddings, Elvis and Priscilla, Frank Sinatra and Mia Farrow and lately the two day marriage of Britney Spears and someone she had just met.

Amongst all the razzmatazz, we were reminded that more than six years on, America is still grieving. Outside the New York New York Hotel (its acronym is NY2) there is a large replica of the Statue of Liberty and at the base, a memorial area where tourists place flags, flowers and messages of sympathy in a moving tribute to the victims of September 11th.

But the lifeblood of Las Vegas has to keep flowing and gambling is a 24-hour a day, all year round business. There is no place else in the world that offers the variety and quantity of gambling games. You have to remember that every hotel, every attraction, every one of the galaxy of neon lights is paid for directly by the millions of gamblers who don't go home with the dollars they arrived with.

And who could go to Las Vegas and not have a little flutter? It would be difficult not to. Our room at the Stardust had all the usual free toiletries and even disposable fluffy slippers, yet the TV had two very poor channels and there were no coffee making facilities. It was obvious. They didn't want us relaxing in our room. They wanted us down there in the casino where there are no windows, no clocks and very few exit signs and the temperature and lighting are constant so the serious gambler will have no distractions.

Scantily clad waitresses cruise between the gaming tables offering gamblers free drink, although they will expect at least a few dollars tip. (Like everywhere else in the States, tipping of at least 15% is compulsory …unless you have a waiting car to take you out of town fast! Also requiring to be tipped in Las Vegas are bartenders, dealers at the games tables, doormen, porters, lift boys, maids and pool attendants, washroom cleaners, the desk clerk, taxi drivers and even ushers in the theatre. In fact, almost everybody.)

If you have never gambled before, the slot machines are mind numbingly simple and the frequent thunderous noise of falling chips into the metal troughs is encouraging. The delighted squeal of two old ladies made me smile but the grim-faced addict furiously playing for hours on a credit card driven 'slot' with the card attached to his waist by a chain, was a depressing sight.

At many places, bingo and scratch cards are offered while you enjoy a $10 'eat all you want' dinner, but the other gambling games are intimidating. It would take a brave novice to approach the sophisticated roulette table or the fast and furious game of craps. But this is not a problem. Every morning, when the haggard addicts have finally found their way out of the casinos, new gamblers are offered free lessons in whatever game takes their fancy. Who knows? Amongst those 34 million tourists, there may be a few who will become high rollers, those charismatic dudes who arrive in stretch limos, swagger their way to the tables and flaunt their wealth by appearing unconcerned at losing thousands.

The Stardust had its little joke. Downstairs in the casino, hundreds of slot machines were ringing and flashing and outside millions of coloured neon lights could probably be seen from outer space, but on our dressing table was a card. It read, 'In the interest of energy conservation, please ensure that you extinguish the light before leaving the room.'

Las Vegas reinvents itself all the time. To our amazement, a month after our visit, we read that the Stardust was to be demolished. Once the ultimate in luxury and style and a favourite haunt of Frank Sinatra, it was now forty-eight years old and in Las Vegas time, that is very old. In its place will be the Echelon, a hotel/casino even bigger and more spectacular than the Wynn, at an estimated cost is $4 billion.

There are no half measures about Las Vegas. You'll either love it or hate it, but you must see it. I'm not saying you should stay long… in fact, I'm begging you not to. Not if you want to go home with a shirt on your back! For Las Vegas cannot hide its motive. It wants your money. But it also wants you to have a great time and you most certainly will.

So that's only fair, isn't it?

The author and her husband spent four days in Las Vegas as part of a 28 day tour of California and Arizona arranged by Saga Holidays.

A Tourist's Prayer

Heavenly Father, look down on me, your humble tourist servant, who is wandering in your New World, taking photographs, sending postcards and wearing shorts, when in thy wisdom, Lord, you designed me with stumpy legs.

In this alien land, protect me from locals who know not where the toilets are but expect me to know their great aunt in Edinburgh.

Give me this day, your divine guidance in choosing which of the creams, shampoos, teabags and plastic pens I may remove from my hotel rooms without violating your eighth commandment.

Lead me, Lord, to inexpensive restaurants, where there are no hamburgers or fried chicken wings and where I can pay for the wine by the glass, not the whole vineyard.

Give me the wisdom to tip correctly. Forgive me for under tipping out of ignorance, but protect me from over-tipping arrogant waiters whose lips curl at anything less than 20%.

Give me the strength to visit all the museums, cathedrals, parks and gardens listed as 'musts' in my tourist guide book. And, if perchance, I miss a historic monument in order to have a nap after lunch, have mercy on me, O Lord, for my flesh is weak.

Dear Lord, keep me from shopping malls and buying gaudy souvenirs which will go to the first jumble sale back home. Lead me not into temptation for I know not what I do.

Almighty Lord, keep my husband from staring at foreign ladies in itsy-bit shorts and comparing their legs with mine. Save him from making a fool of himself and forgetting that he is seventy. Above all, do **not** forgive him his trespasses for he knows **exactly** what he does.

I beseech you, O Lord, to see that my plane is not hijacked and the passenger in the next seat is not thirty stone. And hear me when I cry to thee if my suitcase goes to China.

And when, at last, my journey is over, grant me the favour of finding someone who will listen to my stories of the wondrous things which I have seen.

And finally, Lord, grant my friends the patience to wait until I have transferred my photographs from my digital camera to my computer and let me rejoice in their delight as they view all 500 of them. Only then, will I know that my travels have not been in vain.

Amen, Amen

New York, New York

(published in the *Press and Journal* 22 November, 1995)

I have to say that my idea of a good holiday used to be seeing plays in Pitlochry or golfing at Gairloch, but retirement makes a girl adventurous-like.

So when the advert for the very first flight to New York out of Aberdeen Airport appeared in the *Press And Journal,* my 'game for anything' friends and I were right there, camped on the doorstep of the *Paper Shop* in Union Street with credit cards at the ready, waiting for it to open.

Tickets secured, I enjoyed showing off about it. "Cancel my papers for the weekend. I'm just popping over the Pond to the Big Apple on Friday," had my newsagent mightily impressed.

The planning was fun. It's smart to travel light (on the outward journey at least) so with one curling brush between the six of us and the wardrobe of a plucked Thanksgiving turkey, we took hand luggage only. We thought that our bum-bags, which were so fashionable in the summer, might raise a few eyebrows when worn under a winter coat by ladies of our age.

But in Manhattan, among the human torrent pouring in and out of every shop, office block and bank, you might just get a second glance if you had two heads.

A P&J holiday means you are going away with your chums—all 233 of them. The noise of chatter and laughter in Aberdeen Airport at 8am was deafening and our send-off was quite over the top.

Before we could say "Air 2000" we were up and away, overfed and spoilt rotten by the wonderful cabin crew. Our hotel in New York was the Walcott, the cheapest option. Our room was in need of a paint and the plumbing roared like a furnace, but the bed and bathroom were clean and comfortable.

We could hear the roar of the traffic and the wail of NYPD sirens all night. It seems as if New Yorkers have a total disregard for sleep. Union Street in Aberdeen at the rush hour is a quiet country lane compared to Manhattan streets. But getting from one side of the street is surprisingly easy. The lights say 'walk' or 'don't walk.' Simple, you either get mown down by a stretch limo and go home in a flat pack or you live to spend another dollar.

Five minutes from our hotel and we were on Fifth Avenue. Wow! This was all I had imagined and more. Around 57th Street my credit card was as powerless as my library card. This is where the seriously rich hang out in the mega-glitzy perfumed air of Cartier, Gucci and Tiffany's.

The shop assistants here are not the 'have a nice day, missing you already' types we had encountered earlier on. To get a smile from these girls, your arms need to be hanging out of the sockets with the weight of gold bangles, and your face needs to be lifted high and secured at the top with a knot. One look at my retired face and Marks and Spencers jacket told all there was to know about my financial status.

Just a few blocks north of 5th Avenue is Harlem which we visited on our Sunday excursion. I was rather disturbed by the juxtaposition of the plywood curtain slums of Harlem and the $4 million flats of 5th Avenue. But what I thought would be a depressing look at other people's misery turned out to be one of the highlights of the weekend.

We visited Mount Shiloh Baptist Church and I was privileged to spend an hour at their Thanksgiving Service. Never have I felt so emotionally uplifted as we sang and clapped our way through "Count Your Blessings One By One" with these warm and welcoming people with their powerfully rich voices.

The graceful spire of the Empire State Building was only a block away from our hotel. The skyscraper is about one third of the entire length of Union Street. We zoomed up to the top with the speed of Apollo 13 and it was freezing.

Higher than even the Empire State Building are the 1,350 feet twin towers of the World Trade Centre. It has more than 20,000 windows which are cleaned by American Indians who apparently have a remarkable head for heights. These buildings are only two of a family of giants soaring up to touch the stars.

On Monday we had dinner at the Lighthouse restaurant in New Jersey and gazed at the twinkling Manhattan skyline and felt the breathtaking magic of it all.

The Statue of Liberty is a stirring sight. The giant green lady looks out over the ocean and was a symbol of hope and freedom for the seventeen million immigrants who entered the great melting pot of the United States. I learned at school the poem by Emma Lazurus:

> "Give me your tired, your poor
> Your huddled masses
> Yearning to break free."

We had a whistle stop tour through Chinatown. We wandered for a while among the exotica of the food displayed in the street and absorbed the bustling energy of this area, where New Yorkers love to eat. But in one window I saw dried green lizards for making soup and I felt faintly ill.

On Monday my chums and I relaxed in Central Park by hiring Ed and his horse Guiness to take us on a coach ride to see the sights in this vast green area which keeps New Yorkers sane. Even on a Monday morning it was bustling with joggers, cyclists and dog walkers and in mid November still retained its autumn colours.

You can eat any time, day or night in New York; Italian, Jewish, Chinese. But we went for typical American brunch food, burgers, salads, muffins, bagels and eggs. A monumental plate of food at the deli costs less than five dollars and they pour you coffee by the bucketful.

Speaking for the rest of the pioneers, I think we had an exceptional holiday. I arrived back in Aberdeen with parcels in each hand, round my neck and between my teeth.

I am now in the throes of jet lag. My metabolism is seeking revenge for the scant hours of sleep I allowed myself over the long weekend.

But as Frank Sinatra sings, "Start Spreading The News...." New York is wonderful!

Six

Researched Articles

A Sinister Way of Life

(Published in *The Lady*)

'Sinister' is not usually an adjective you would use to describe a happy little toddler. But, even at age two, it applied to me. Yet I am a decent sort of person. I feed the birds, give to charity, and when I chase the cat next door, there really isn't murder in my heart. I am merely dextrously challenged, one of a forgotten and often ridiculed 10% of the population who is left-handed.

The lives of left-handers throughout history have not been easy. Almost every culture, because of superstition and narrow-mindedness, has reacted adversely. The ancient Greeks regarded the left side as unlucky and two and a half thousand years later, certain casinos in Las Vegas refuse to employ left-handed dealers as some punters have the same suspicions.

All the world religions have been defiantly right-handed. In Arab countries and among Hindus, the left hand was used for personal hygiene and nothing else. Today's more educated Arabs have a more relaxed attitude but the taboo still exists in India. In fundamentalist Islamic cultures the left hand is still associated with evil. When the Muslim spiritual leader, the Ayatollah Khomeini, toppled the Shah of Iran from power in 1979, he whipped up a frenzy among the screaming masses by announcing that the Shah was cursed by Allah, because his first born son was left-handed.

The Christian faith is also tainted by anti-sinistrality. According to an early biographer of St George, he showed an antipathy for anything sinister at a very tender age by refusing to suckle at his mother's left breast.

The Bible is peppered with phrases such as "the strong right arm

68

of God," and "sitting at God's right hand." And during the last supper, guess what side of Jesus, Judas was *not* sitting at?

At her trial, Joan of Arc was adamant that her 'voices' came from the right and therefore from God. But her enemies had seen her in battle with the sword in her left hand and that, of course, guaranteed her fate. She was burned as a witch in the market place at Rouen in 1431.

Left-hand taboos applied in many primitive societies and survived into the middle of the 20th century. An account in the July 1965 National Geographic magazine tells of African tribal women in the Lower Niger who were forbidden to use the left hand for cooking. Those who disobeyed this rule were branded as witches. Any child in the tribe who showed the slightest sign of being left-handed was subjected to the most appalling cruelty. The offending hand was boiled until it was so mutilated that it was permanently useless.

If that is unbelievably barbaric, anti-left atrocities were being carried out in Scottish schools until quite recently. When I was a child in the 1940's the practice of a painful rap to a tiny knuckle with the blackboard pointer was common and the practice of tethering the arm to the back of the seat had only just disappeared into the annals of Scottish educational history.

I remember wanting desperately to be good at cutting out shapes but I never understood why my scissors refused to do the job which others found so easy. I had a terrible time with dip pens and ink. For a start, the inkwell was at the right side of the desk. Then the nib would dig into the paper as I pushed it across the page, (right-handers *pull* the pen) and the final misery came when my hand moved on and smudged it all. My teachers complained in every report about my clumsiness and messy work. I never knew why I was lacking in dexterity. I didn't even notice that I wrote with my left hand and the other children did not. The ultimate insult was when one teacher wrote, "Elizabeth has two left hands...and two left feet."

In the modern classroom, things have changed very little. Mrs Gillian Shepherd, Secretary of State for Education from 1995-1997, made the astonishing statement, "Left-handedness is not recognised as a special educational need within the meaning of the Education Acts. The Department does not collect information on what proportion of pupils is left-handed nor on whether being left-handed has an impact on likely educational achievement." It would appear that there are one million left-handed children currently in primary and secondary schools not being catered for or appropriately supported.

This also applies to universities and colleges. My young dentist, who writes with the typical left-handers' claw, told me that when he was a student he had to "improvise" at a right handed dental work station. Now in his own practice, his pride and joy is his state of the art ambidextrous surgery.

However, things are improving slowly. All major banks are now following the lead of Lloyds TSB, who for quite some time, have boldly gone where no bank has gone before and produced left-handed cheque-books with the stubs on the right side

Then I discovered, more than fifty years too late, a full range of left-handed implements including scissors, pens, knives, irons, potato peelers and even a computer keyboard in a wonderful Aladdin's cave for lefties in Central London and my clumsiness disappeared overnight. My writing has improved, my typing speed is phenomenal, I can cut out paper shapes as neatly as my grandson and I can peel a potato without reducing it to the size of a garden pea. The shop has everything a lefty ever dreamed of. Even if your boomerang won't come back because its aerofoil is on the wrong side, then look no further than *Anything Left-handed* at 57 Brewer Street, London, W1F 9UL. The shop also provides a worldwide mail order service.

With specially adapted equipment, left-handers do well in sports. Thirty per cent of the world's top tennis players are left-handed. In fact, right-handers fear the spin coming from a left hand racquet. In cricket, the great Sir Gary Sobers batted and bowled the wrong way round whilst in fencing, bowls and boxing, southpaws even have certain advantages. Fair enough about polo, though. For reasons of safety to both pony and rider, it is against the rules to play this game left-handed.

Although some do exist, specially adapted instruments for left-handed musicians are either claimed to be impossible to make or prohibitively expensive. A conductor friend joked that a left-handed string player would look odd in an orchestra and would literally get right up the noses of fellow players. In today's society, so politically correct in all matters racial, religious and sexual, would he have dared to suggest that an obese person or a musician in a wheelchair or a Muslim clarinettist, dressed in a hijab, would also stand out and spoil the symmetry of the group?

Throughout the ages, all sorts of reasons have been given for left-handedness. Certain facts have been proved. More boys than girls are left handed. There is a high incidence in twins although usually only one is left-handed as is the case with my twin granddaughters. And, like me, left-handers are often the offspring of older mothers. Statistics also show that left handedness among children brain damaged at birth is thirty per cent, three times the normal figure.

In 400 BC, Plato blamed careless handling by nursing mothers for the condition. They failed to swaddle their infants tightly enough, thus allowing the offending limb to stray out of the blanket and become dominant.

As late as 1946, Dr Abram Blau, chief psychiatrist at the New York University Clinic, said that sinistrality was the behaviour of a truculent child who used his left hand for the sheer hell of it and usually came from an emotionally deprived home. Freud went further and suggested that this wilfulness sometimes took the extreme form of bowel retention. (I was the much cherished only child of the best parents in the world, but now I remember that my mother did sometimes give me a dose of syrup of figs ... ...)

The modern theory is that handedness is all to do with the brain. The right hemisphere, dominant in left-handers, controls memory, emotions and concrete thinking. You might therefore expect a left hander to be intuitive and mystical with a strong visual sense. Leonardo da Vinci had a bad start in life. He was left-handed and illegitimate. Yet he was the greatest creative genius of all time and the very personification of the Renaissance.

Other geniuses we can claim are Bach, Picasso and Einstein.

There are a *few* black sheep. Jack the Ripper and the Boston Strangler were left-handers. So is Osama bin Laden.

I am now happy to be a lefty. It makes me feel special and it's part of my identity. Life on the left side is, in fact, …. *All right.*

Ten Years Gone but Not Forgotten

(Published in the *Highlander*, the *Leopard* and the bicentenary edition of *The Tiger and Sphinx*. There were great photographs with the original magazine articles.)

Ten years ago, grown men and women in the north east of Scotland were weeping unashamedly in the streets as the drums and pipes of the 1st Battalion Gordon Highlanders 'beat retreat' for the last time and said farewell to the towns and villages which were their former recruitment areas.

For on September 17th, 1994, the Gordon Highlanders amalgamated with the Queen's Own Highlanders as part of sweeping defence cuts. This decision brought a storm of fierce protest from all corners of the world, and left mixed senses of pride, outrage, grief and betrayal.

This was a particularly bitter blow, as only three months before, this proud regiment had celebrated the 200th birthday of their founding in 1794 by the 4th Duke of Gordon to fight in the Napoleonic Wars. However, it is Jean, the beautiful Duchess of Gordon, who is best remembered. She toured the north-east of Scotland and kissed every man who accepted the King's Shilling to enlist. This appealed to the naturally romantic nature of the Scots and the regiment of 1000 men was formed in a matter of days.

The Gordons served with the highest distinction in many campaigns during the 200 years of their proud and mighty history. Arguably, the Regiment's greatest triumph was the Battle of Waterloo on June 18th, 1815, which brought peace in Europe after many years of war. Although reduced to about 200 men after the Battle of Quatre Bras, only a few days before, the 92nd Regiment, under the command of Lieutenant Colonel Macdonald forced a way with their bayonets through the solid 3000-strong column of Napoleon's Imperial Guard. The French were panic-stricken as the kilted, bagpipe-skirling Highlanders charged at them with savage ferocity, and they began to lay down their arms. Then the Royal Scots Greys rode up to reinforce the charge of the Gordons. Infantry and cavalry cheered each other on, shouting, 'Scotland for ever and second to none!' Many of the soldiers caught hold of the horses' legs and stirrups to support them as they surged forward to complete the rout, taking 1900 prisoners. The death toll for the Highlanders was 82.

In the 20th century, the Regiment fought in the two World Wars. They were so feared by the enemy that the German High Command placed the regiment at the top of the 'black list' of dangerous formations.

The close-knit communities of the northeast of Scotland lost thousands of their men folk in the unparalleled horror of the Somme in July 1916. The slaughter was beyond belief but among the screams of the mortally wounded, machine gun fire and the whistling of rifle bullets, in the darkness from some stinking dug-out or of a mud filled trench, was the sound of bagpipes. A lone piper was playing 'Highland Laddie' (the regimental march of the Gordons until 1932) and as in days of old, the martial music of Scotland was preparing her sons for attack. There was many a German who would be sorry that he ever heard of these 'kilted tigers from Hell.'

In the Second World War, in the early summer of 1940, the Gordon Highlanders were part of the 51st Highland Division, fighting in the same part of northern France. By the end of May, Belgium and Holland had surrendered to the Nazis and British troops were fighting a desperate rearguard action on the French coast around Dunkirk as the German troops moved in to surround them. More and more men including the Gordon Highlanders were thrown into the fight but the great German war machine continued to advance, wave after wave, sparing no-one. On June 4th over 300,000 British troops were brought back to Britain in Operation Dynamo, the great evacuation of Dunkirk, when every conceivable kind of boat from pleasure cruisers to small fishing smacks took part in the rescue. Unfortunately there were many more who didn't make it. For the Scots in particular it was a terrible disaster, a second Flodden, felt right across Scotland. The Gordon Highlanders, true to their tradition, had fought to the last round, but many were killed, and even more were captured and held in prisoner of war camps for the rest of the war.

But the 51st was destined to live again and the division was quickly reformed with duplicate battalions from regiments that were to form the roll call of Scotland's military history. The Gordons rallied to win battle honours at El Alamein. In the long 13 day battle at Alamein, the gallant Highlanders were where you would expect them to be, at the front and in the thick of it, driving Rommel into retreat. They were as brave and tenacious in the blistering heat of the Western Desert as they had been in the freezing mud of the Somme. And still the pipers played the old tunes of the homeland lifting the hearts of the soldiers, stirring them to victory.

There are those who would laugh at the music of the bagpipes. But let them march behind a piper of the Gordon Highlanders as he plays the powerfully evocative 'Cock O' the North' and they will know the magic of this music, which has so great an appeal to Scottish hearts.

The most famous piper of all was Piper George Findlater who won the Victoria Cross for his outstanding heroism during the storming of the Heights of Dargai during the Afghan War in 1897. Although both his ankles were shattered by bullets, he continued to play 'Cock O' the North' and the battle march so inspired his comrades that they routed the Afghans from their secure position and thus defeated them. It took the kilted warriors just half an hour to complete the task, which the other British troops had failed to do in over five hours. On his return home, Piper Findlater received the Victoria Cross from Queen Victoria herself.

In the second half of the 20th century, the Gordon Highlanders continued to serve throughout the world, taking pride in their peace-keeping role in Malaya, Cyprus, Kenya, Zanzibar, Swaziland, Borneo, Berlin, Northern Ireland and Bosnia. They also played their part in the successful completion of the Gulf War.

Sir Thomas Moore, who died at Corunna in 1809, and in whose memory the Gordon Highlanders wore black buttons on their spats, said, "It is the principles of integrity and moral correctness that I admire most in Highland soldiers."

These sentiments have prevailed throughout the years. In 1949, the City of Aberdeen awarded the Gordons with the top civic honour, 'The Freedom of the City.'

On that occasion, the Duke of Gloucester said, "The Regiment will always uphold the fine tradition and stand steadfast like the granite from which this beautiful city is built."

But now the bugler has sounded 'The Last Post' and our proud Regiment has gone. On 17th September, ten years ago, the commanding officers of the Gordons and The Queen's Own Highlanders met at the Telford Bridge, Craigellachie, the bridge which traditionally marked the border of their recruitment grounds, and toasted their amalgamation with a large dram of malt whisky.

But the Gordon Highlanders, who won 19 Victoria Crosses, more than any other infantry regiment in the British Army, will forever be in the memories of the people who originate from the northeast of Scotland.

George Wishart (1513-1546)

The Martyr from Montrose

(This article was published in the *Leopard* and the *Highlander.*)

R eligious belief mattered very much to the people of Scotland in the 16th Century. Many were no longer satisfied with the way in which the all-powerful Church of Rome conducted its affairs.

Senior churchmen were obscenely rich, but hunger and disease hung darkly over the pitiful lives of ordinary folk. Often the only cow, or the very coat off their backs, was the price they had to pay for a Christian burial.

Bishops and priests had taken vows of celibacy, but John Hamilton, Archbishop of St Andrews, had seven illegitimate children, and other grand prelates were not free from blame. The infamous Cardinal David Beaton, an ambitious and ruthless man, lived with Marion Ogilvie, daughter of Lord Ogilvie of Airlie, and their daughter and two sons, but he had at least six other historically traceable children.

High ranking churchmen and their offspring took over church buildings and lands for their own profit. Uneducated priests, who not only knew no Latin, but could barely read nor write, were paid a pittance to perform necessary religious duties.

At this time also, there was no one on the throne of Scotland. King James V had died a few weeks after the Battle of Solway Moss and King Henry VIII already had plans to make Scotland part of England.

During these troubled years there were devout men who believed that the Roman Catholic Church was too corrupt to reform itself and that it had moved too far away from the teachings of Christ.

One such man was a tall, good-looking Scot who was born on the outskirts of Montrose in 1513. Son of an educated upper class landowner, George Wishart went to Montrose Grammar School and King's College, Aberdeen. Scotland's first Education Act, in 1496 ordered every substantial landowner to send his eldest son to school and university. George was a brilliant scholar and in 1538 he returned to his old school to teach Greek.

Montrose merchants had close links with the continent and illegally imported copies of the Greek New Testament found their way into the classroom. These books were circulated and read avidly.

George Wishart was an inspired teacher and preacher. Before long, the ordinary citizens of Montrose were gathering to hear the young man protest that the Bible should be the only source of belief for Christians. He rejected all other beliefs not supported by the New Testament. These protestations were dangerous because they contradicted the teaching of the Roman Catholic Church.

He translated into Scots another contraband book, which he titled *The Confession of the Faith of the Swezerland*. This document was revolutionary, as it emphasised that the only head of the Church was Christ, whose officers were ministers. There should only be two sacraments, Holy Communion and baptism, and importantly, it was the duty of the civil authorities to defend true religion. The Protestant reformers in Europe, where these new ideas were coming from, were regarded as heretics and Wishart's unorthodox preaching was attracting the unfavourable attention of Cardinal David Beaton.

Young Wishart was forced to flee to Cambridge University where for a time he was safe and where his beliefs were reinforced by like-minded friends.

He also spent time in Switzerland, where Protestantism was moving ahead rapidly under the enlightened ministry of John Calvin.

However by 1544, he was back in Scotland. Under his evangelical leadership, the people of Montrose were amongst the first to give strong support to the Reformation.

In the months that followed, huge crowds in plague-ridden Dundee flocked to his meetings. Perhaps he had a sense of the shortness of his own time, but it became more and more urgent for him to spread his teachings further afield.

By this time, Wishart had been joined by John Knox, a young man from Haddington, who had renounced his priestly duties and had become an ardent supporter. Wishart's zeal made him fearless and careless about his own safety, but John Knox carried a two-handed sword to protect his friend.

In early 1546, he was invited to travel to Edinburgh to meet with the nobles, Cassillis and Glencairn, to discuss the possibility of finding a way to bring some peace between the Reformers and the Roman Catholic Church.

But Wishart never got to Edinburgh. Knowing his freedom was short lived, he urged John Knox to go home saying "One is sufficient for a sacrifice."

On Cardinal Beaton's orders, he was arrested and transferred to St Andrews Castle. Although this was the home of supposedly holy men, St Andrews Castle housed the notorious Bottle Dungeon. This was the most gruesome of all dungeons in any Scottish stronghold….and Scotland had some horrible ones indeed!

Prisoners were thrown into the narrow neck of the dungeon to the floor 24 feet below. In freezing darkness with water dripping off the rock walls, they lay in their own filth, surviving on whatever scraps of food was lowered through the hole above. No one ever escaped from its hellish depths and those who died there were flung into the sea.

George Wishart spent many days there whilst Cardinal Beaton arranged for him to be charged and found guilty of heresy and burned at the stake. He was determined that by publicly defeating and ridiculing Wishart, the new religion would be finally squashed.

On 28 February, Wishart was removed from the dungeon to attend his trial in St Andrews cathedral. Although Wishart swore that he had only been preaching the word of God, Beaton saw him as a dangerous adversary and even suggested that Wishart was an agent of the English crown, which of course, would have been treason.

Beaton's evil rhetoric was persuasive but Wishart was pronounced guilty only of heresy.

On the following day, as Cardinal Beaton watched in cushioned splendour from the warmth and luxury of his castle drawing-room, George Wishart was led out bound and chained. He walked with courage and dignity. He was forgiving and magnanimous in his death, kissing the cheek of the lowly servant who was struggling to keep the faggots alight on that rain-swept day on the first day of March, 1546.

The crowds who watched his patient endurance as the flames claimed his body, were deeply moved. He was now a martyr who did more for the new faith by his dying than he could ever have done in his life.

Two months later, avengers of Wishart's death murdered the Cardinal and hung his body over the wall of the castle suspended by one foot and one hand. He had died a coward, begging that he should not be hurt as he was a priest. His body was preserved in salt and flung into his own fearsome rock pit, and only given proper burial one year later in Blackfriars Chapel.

George Wishart would not have approved of this revengeful violence. He had been an evangelist who always pursued the gospel of peace. It is unlikely that he took any part in the political entanglement of the period.

After Beaton's death, the Protestant movement went underground for a few years. It wasn't until 1559, under the leadership of John Knox, that the authority of the Pope in Scotland officially ended. The practice of Mass was made illegal and the institution of the new Church of Scotland was established.

But it was George Wishart who had so courageously laid its foundations.

Alexander Burnes
Soldier, Traveller, Writer, Montrosian

(Published in the *Highlander* and the *Leopard*)

James Burnes, twice Provost of Montrose between 1818 and 1825, was very proud of his family connection with Robert Burns. The poet's uncle was Provost Burnes' grandfather. But, he too, had a distinguished family; the most famous being his fourth son, Alexander.

Young Alexander showed little academic promise, attending the Trade School instead of the more prestigious Montrose Academy. He was fortunate that his father had some clout and was able to pull a string or two to secure for him a cadetship with the Honourable East India Company. So in 1821, chaperoned by his elder brother James, who was to begin a distinguished career as a doctor in Bombay, the 16 year-old lad left Montrose for the long sea journey to India.

India had an immediate and mysterious attraction for Alexander. He learned all he could about local customs and manners and discovered an amazing flair for languages. Within six months he had mastered Persian, Hindi and Arabic and gained quick promotion in his work as an interpreter and translator.

Very soon his work was taking him far away from military quarters. His detailed reports of his journeys to the delta of the Indus in the Arabian Sea and later, to the northwest frontier of Cutch, greatly impressed his superiors.

Then in 1830 Alexander was chosen to carry out an unusual mission. The ruler of the Punjab, in north west British India, the Maharajah Runjit Singh, had sent King William IV some valuable

Kashmir shawls. Anxious to maintain the good relationship, the British government pondered about an appropriate reciprocal gift. In their wisdom they decided that five dray horses would be exactly right for a fabulously rich and powerful maharajah.

The stallion and four mares survived the six-month sea journey from England. The rest of the task was to be left to the young officer, Alexander Burnes.

About two-thirds of the vast Indian sub continent was officially under British rule, but much of it was unexplored. Journeys across desert and through jungle, which now take only a few hours by air, were long, arduous and dangerous. So to escort the horses 1000 miles overland would have been impossible. To give the mission any chance of success, the only alternative was to go by river craft all the way up the Indus with only a short land march on to Lahore, the capital of the Punjab.

However the mission had a dual purpose. Whilst ostensibly escorting the horses, Burnes was also required to survey the Indus and check how far it was navigable for trade and military purposes and to report on 'various other particulars in which full information was highly desirable'... in other words, to spy out the land. So Burnes, accompanied by personally chosen travelling companions and a full retinue of servants, and, of course, the enormous dray horses, set off in early 1831 on their expedition up the River Indus, starting from a port in Cutch.

However in the north and northwest of Cutch is the state of Sind, which had not yet been conquered and annexed by Great Britain. The Sindis were hostile towards the travellers and for two months refused to allow them to sail further upstream. During this time they were threatened by barbaric tribesmen and half their craft were destroyed by gales. Eventually, after a stern letter to the Emir from the British Resident in Cutch, they were allowed to go....but only after the Emir had picked through his presents and arranged to exchange the gold watch and crystal candlesticks for something more to his liking. In his reports, it was obvious that Burnes despised the Sindis. He found them barbaric, greedy and dirty. Even the wretched beggars who stuffed sand and mud into their mouths failed to evoke his sympathy.

At last, six months after setting out, the travellers reached friendly territory. They were warmly welcomed by a reception party sent ahead by the Maharajah Runjit Singh and ten days later they were escorted into Lahore.

Fortunately the Maharajah was delighted with his present. With sentiments which were a touch over flowery even by oriental standards, he said, "These animals surpass the horses of every country in the world. When the new moon beheld the size of their shoes, it turned pale with envy and nearly disappeared from the sky."

The Maharajah was a stunted, one-eyed monster. He was an alcoholic who performed the extremes of cruelty and debauchery. He was a despot who routinely mutilated anyone who displeased him. Yet in his way, he was a wise and able ruler and the British Government respected him. He and the young man from Montrose established a curious rapport and they spent many hours in conversation. Burnes and his party spent two months as the Maharajah's guest, enjoying his lavish hospitality. When it was time to go they were laden with fabulous gifts.

On his return journey he met with the exiled king of Kabul, Shah Shujah. The man did not impress Burnes and this encounter was to shape his political career at the end of his life. But meanwhile Burnes was flying high. The detailed reports of his successful mission were noted in high places. Burnes was in Delhi, being presented to the Mogul Emperor, when he received a written commendation for his work. Approval was granted for his next adventure, a journey into central Asia, to the countries bordering the River Oxus, over the mountains to Bokhara and the Caspian Sea beyond.

As it happened, Burnes' travelling ambitions coincided with the British Government's concern about possible Russian activity in that area. The intelligent young officer was exactly the right man to find out what was going on.

This time they were leaving from Delhi, so the journey back to Lahore with his new party of friends and servants was short and uneventful. Of course, he had first to seek permission. He enjoyed showing the Maharajah that he could match him in oriental hyperbole. He wrote, "It would add to my happiness to renew my terms of friendship with a prince whose exalted virtues filled me with recollections of perpetual delight."

Runjit Singh was pleased to welcome Burnes again and his hospitality was even more magnificent. Burnes rode in a golden howdah on top of a richly caparisoned elephant. On a hunting trip, his tent was furnished with Kashmir rugs and embroidered satin cushions and the sheets on his camp bed were of yellow silk. He was lavishly entertained in the palace, but the young officer did not always like what he saw. In his notebook Burnes recorded his disgust at the cruel sport of baiting and slaughtering wild boar. Nor did he share the Maharajah's delight in goading inebriated dancing girls to wrestle and tear each other's hair out, for his pleasure.

After a month Burnes was given permission to continue his journey. They had a terrifying experience crossing the Indus when it was in spate and one of his party and a few horses were drowned. But in Peshawar at the east end of the Kyber Pass, they were welcomed by the young Sultan Mohammed Khan, definitely a family man who already had thirty concubines in his harem and about sixty children. He wasn't sure of the exact number!

The Sultan gave Burnes a letter of introduction to Dost Mohammed Khan, the ruler of Kabul, but also the most powerful man in Afghanistan. Over endless cups of tea, with added salt and fat, he questioned Burnes about a wide range of subjects, from British taxation to Watt's steam engine, from European music to the price of British goods. He praised Burnes' fluency in his language and approved his decision to discard western dress.

The next stage of the journey over the vast mountain range of the Hindu Kush was to be hazardous in the extreme and Burnes and his party made careful preparations for the dangers ahead. They jettisoned all but their most essential equipment, disguised themselves as paupers and joined up with a caravan of other travellers. They were careful not only to dress like the others, but also to get the customs and religious observances right. This was territory where normal relations between human beings did not exist. Their apparent poverty might prevent them from being robbed but they were even more likely to be captured for the vast slave market or be tortured and executed as non-believers. Bands of tribesmen whose religious fanaticism bordered on insanity, scoured the area. If, for example, they had discovered someone asleep with his feet pointing towards Mecca, they would have cut the throats of the entire party. They survived almost unscathed because Burnes had the foresight to hire a wise old man called Hyat to be their cafila-bashee, the spokesman and organiser of the route. He turned out to be the most trustworthy of men and rescued them from many difficult situations. Meanwhile Burnes continued to record every detail, sometimes crouched in the pannier of his camel as they crossed the scorching desert, sometimes in the dark and freezing cold as the rest of the caravan slept.

At the end of June, 1832, after six months of travel, the party all recovering from malaria, reached their destination, Bokhara. The city, situated in an oasis and surrounded by desert, was founded by Alexander the Great in the 4th Century B.C. Both prosperity and ruin had touched Bokhara in its long history. Along with Samarkand, it was on one of the main trading routes of the ancient world. It was totally destroyed by the notorious Mongul conqueror Genghiz Khan in 1220 but when Marco Polo visited the city at the end of that century, it had been rebuilt. In 1832 it appeared to be a very holy city with 366 religious academies and numerous splendid mosques, which contrasted with the hovels where most of the people lived. The population was 150,000, of whom three-quarters were Persian slaves. The Emir was suspicious of strangers, with good reason. He feared the expansion of British India from the south and Russia from the north. In fact Bokhara was conquered in 1866 by Tsarist Russia and later became part of the Soviet Republic.

At first the travellers were refused entry into the city and their baggage was searched on several occasions by unfriendly officials. However Burnes wrote a letter of introduction to the Koosh Begee, or principal minister, including the plethora of sycophantic greetings, 'Oh, Tower of Islam, Pillar of all Wisdom, Gem of the Faith,' et cetera, and they were escorted into the city….on foot, of course. No infidel was allowed to ride within the city wall. Burnes was closely interrogated by the minister about his personal status and the purpose of his visit. His replies (and the gift of a compass) must have satisfied the minister, because he was allowed to move unmolested through the streets. But he was careful to keep a low profile and obey all the rules. Although he caught glimpses of the Emir Nasrullah Bahadur Khan going to the Great Kalyan Mosque for midday prayers, Burnes was not granted an audience. This was probably fortunate as the Emir was a bloodthirsty and sadistic madman, who among numerous other atrocities, axed his chief artillery man in half. It was considered a major crime to be the 'wrong' type of Muslim. The Emir was a Sunni Muslim, so Shiah Muslims lay shackled in noxious prison cells without sanitation. But for those whom the emir took a particular dislike to, there was the Pit, a dark twenty-foot cylindrical hole full of rats and scorpions, truly the inspiration of an evil mind. Another landmark in the city was the Kalyan minaret or the Tower of Death. Faithless wives were thrown from the top. No man was allowed up there as he might spy on the palace concubines relaxing on the balcony of their quarters. The Emir therefore had many enemies and was in constant fear of being murdered. He avoided poisoning by having all his food tested by slaves and lived until 1860. His last act of barbarism was to enjoy watching his senior wife being stabbed as he lay in his deathbed.

All the women were in strict purdah, only showing their eyes. Yet Burnes was able to report in his journal that indoors the women wore their hair in long braided tresses, stained their teeth black and wore ornate velvet boots. If this was first hand information, then Burnes was lucky, as a Bokhara husband was entitled to shoot any man who looked at his wives or daughters.

There was another danger, apart from being arrested in the street and dragged before the Emir on some trumped-up charge. Malaria, dysentery and typhoid were endemic and the drinking water harboured diseases like cholera, Bokhara boil, and Guinea worm. In the latter, the three foot long worm grows between the skin and the flesh and tries to emerge through an ulcer at the ankle inch by horrible inch.

So having spent a month in Bokhara, Burnes decided it was time to go. Surprisingly, his document giving permission to depart was signed by the Emir himself.

They joined a caravan of merchants making a party of 150 men and 100 camels and they entered the Turkoman desert. Robber bands of Turkoman tribesmen whose hobby was collecting slaves, were scouring the desert. Once again, because of his remarkable ability to conceal himself amongst his fellow travellers, Burnes' party outwitted the raiders. They emerged from the desert unscathed and also managed to help several fleeing Persian slaves to return to their own country.

In Meshed, the holy city of the Shiah Muslims, Burnes parted from his retinue and headed northwest to the Caspian Sea. But first he met the Crown Prince of Persia who was short of cash to pay his army. Slavery was about to be abolished in the British colonies and since his army was fighting those who captured and enslaved his people, he reckoned that Britain should pay the wages of his soldiers.

At long last, Burnes reached the Caspian Sea where he enjoyed a sail and a dinner of grilled sturgeon. His journey was complete. A ship of the East India Company was waiting for him at Bushire on the Persian Gulf and he hurried south to join it. Five weeks later he was back in Bombay.

After twelve years in India he had accumulated many months of leave. His reception in London was rapturous. He had interviews with the Prime Minister and King William and was pursued by the fashionable London set. He received many public honours, including being made a Fellow of the Royal Society. Later he was given the title of Sir Alexander Burnes.

But his priority was to get his notes in order and get his book written. *Travels into Bokhara* was a best seller and ran into several publications. The fee for the copyright alone would have made him a rich man.

Back home in Montrose his welcome was even more rapturous. The 'Montrose Review' of January 1834 (now in the Montrose

Library archive) reports every detail of the banquet given in his honour. Alexander Burnes, aged twenty-nine, was a celebrity.

Burnes refused all offers of tempting career opportunities and returned to India in 1835. In the following year he was sent back to Kabul to enter commercial relations with his old friend Dost Mohammed. There was great unrest in the country with the threat of invasion from Russia, the Sikhs and the Persians. Burnes reported to his superiors that Dost Mohammed was the only man able to control the unruly chiefs and unite them against their enemies. However the British Government decided to support the exiled king, Shah Shujah, whom Burnes had met on his return journey after delivering the dray horses. Burnes, a good judge of character, considered that the old king was weak and would be unable to influence his turbulent countrymen.

Unfortunately, Burnes' advice was ignored and from then on, the first Afghan War, which began in 1838, lurched from disaster to disaster for Britain.

Burnes had to accept the restoration of Shah Shujah to the throne of Kabul and he became the political resident in the city. The once cautious sensible officer, who knew how to avoid danger, started to behave with incredible stupidity. At his luxurious house in the city he wined and dined and had open affairs with local ladies. He caused important Afghans to lose face and made many enemies. He was increasingly hated and blamed for bringing the British to Afghanistan.

On 21st November, 1841, a mob stormed his house and he, along with his brother Charlie and his entire household of guards and servants, was butchered with long Afghan knives.

Who knows what else this remarkable young man might have achieved? His adventures fired the imagination of the British public all these years ago and Montrosians are justifiably proud of him.

Balnamoon's Cave

(Published in the *Leopard* and the *Highlander.*)

Encircled by mountains, Glen Esk is the most beautiful of all Angus glens. It has the distinction of having been the theatre of many romantic historical events.

Deep in the glen, way beyond the Queen's Well, nestling among the rocks at the foot of the Craig of Doune, is a secret hiding place called Balnamoon's Cave.

James Carnegie, the "rebel laird" of Balnamoon, was one of the best known in a large widespread family of wealthy landowning Carnegies whose family tree can be traced back to the 13th Century. In 1734, he married Margaret Arbuthnott, the heiress of Findowrie, and thereby added large parts of Tannadice and Brechin to his estates.

By the time Prince Charles Edward Stuart arrived in Scotland in July 1745, James and Margaret had five sons and two daughters. But James was still a young man with a yearn for adventure, and family and estate commitments did not deter him from becoming a fervent Jacobite. With his party of retainers, he left his wife and children and joined up with the Camerons, the Macdonalds and all the other clans devoted to helping the Young Chevalier claim the crown of his ancestors.

By September the Jacobite army was 2000 strong. On the 27th of that month, Balnamoon fought his first battle. The Highlanders had marched overnight to surprise and defeat Sir John Cope at Prestonpans. The Highlanders poked fun at Cope in their new marching song.

"Hey, Johnnie Cope, are ye waukin' yet
And are yer drums a' beating yet?
If ye were waukin' I would wait
Tae gang tae the coals in the mornin'."

Flushed with their success in Scotland, the Prince and his army advanced boldly into England, avoiding General Wade in Northumberland and capturing Carlisle.

But many Highlanders had deserted at the Border, there were very few fresh recruits, funds were low and there was no sign of the promised help from France. At Derby, on 4 December, 1745, they halted to take stock of their situation. Charles wanted to march on to London but the army leaders argued their case and said that further advance would be foolish. Eventually, the Prince agreed to a retreat.

Balnamoon remained loyal to the Jacobite cause and when they re-entered Scotland he was in the midst of the fighting at the Battle of Falkirk on 17 January, 1746, when the government troops under General Hawley were soundly defeated.

But then, good fortune left them. As they retreated north, they were pursued by the Duke of Cumberland and his men, who were ready and eager for a final showdown, which took place at Culloden.

This marked the end of the Jacobite ambitions. The Prince said, "Let every man seek his own safety the best way he can," and he himself fled west.

Somehow, Balnamoon struggled the long miles back to Angus, but raiding parties of soldiers scoured the glens with orders that fugitives should be killed, their houses burned and cattle seized.

For many months Balnamoon did not dare go near his home and hid in a small cave about 100 yards above the Water of Mark. It is not easy to spot, as it is well camouflaged by the surrounding rocks. It is hard to imagine anyone living in this tiny damp hole even for a few hours but in spite of the loneliness and terrible discomfort, this cave was Balnamoon's only place of safety for many months. Obviously he could not have survived without the help of loyal friends and many of the locals in the glen not only knew about the cave, but gave him food and shelter in their homes when it was safe to do so.

However, there was a huge price on his head, and the anti-Episcopalian parish minister, John Scott, is said to have alerted the authorities that Balnamoon was in the glen; but he did not know about the cave.

One very cold day, the rebel laird, disguised as a lowly servant, was warming himself by the kitchen fire in a neighbouring farm when a party of soldiers arrived. The quick-witted farmer welcomed the soldiers into his house. As he plied them with food in his kitchen, he spoke roughly to his "lazy servant," ordering him to get back to his work cleaning out the byre. Balnamoon needed no second telling and made off barefoot over the windswept moor to the safety of his cave.

Balnamoon was never caught in the glen but later, after he had left the district, he was eventually arrested and imprisoned in the Tower of London. Amazingly he did not suffer the same fate as his fellow Jacobites. The records say he was set free because of a "misnomer." Did he deny that he was James Carnegie, 6th laird of Balnamoon or did a large sum of money exchange hands?

We will never know, but coincidentally, there was another James Carnegie on the scene at the same time. Sir James Carnegie of Pitarrow was educated at Glasgow University and a highly respected baronet, who was first elected Member of Parliament for Kincardineshire in 1741 and was frequently re-elected. He also fought with distinction at the Battle of Culloden, but on the side of the Duke of Cumberland. It can be imagined that the executioners in the Tower of London were very fearful of beheading the wrong Carnegie! It appeared that Balnamoon was a very lucky man.

Meanwhile, divine retribution was meted out to the informer, John Scott. He was thrown from his horse and died instantly, at the ruins of the Jacobite chapel. The previous year he had been delighted to watch it being torched by government troops.

Eventually, it was safe for Balnamoon to return to his wife and children in Angus and he spent the rest of his days peacefully administering his estates.

The brave farmer who put his own life and property in jeopardy to save the life of the laird was always a welcome guest at the Carnegie family home near Brechin.

Balnamoon's cave is on OS Map 44, MF 395833. But you are quite likely to miss it just as Butcher Cumberland's soldiers did, more than 260 years ago.

Seven

Robert Burns

Ae Fond Kiss

(Published in the P&J and the *Highlander*)

If Robert Burns had been like the rest of us, falling in love, getting married and staying faithful, he would never have written the most tender and beautiful love poems of all time.

Burns felt the first stirrings of love when he was a young lad of fourteen and his earliest surviving verses were for Nelly Kirkpatrick, who worked alongside him at the harvest of 1773. His lines are of admiration and respect for the lovely young girl:

> "But Nelly's looks are blythe and sweet,
> And, what is best of a',
> Her reputation is complete
> And fair without a flaw."

The heady euphoric state of new love encourages even the most prosaic of us to pen a few lines of verse, so Burns' lifelong succession of love affairs meant he was never short of inspiration. He wrote his greatest poems when he was actively head over heels in love and with his shortbread-tin good looks he was welcomed into the arms of one 'lovely dear' after another.

In 1780, when the Tarbolton Bachelors' Club was formed, one of the rules was that each member must be a professed lover of one or more of the female sex, an early statement of Burns' polygamous attitude to women. He wrote,

> "The sweetest hours that e'er I spent
> Are spent among the lassies, O."

Furiously loving the women and loved by them in return, there weren't many pretty Ayrshire lassies who escaped his amorous attentions and most of his loves he immortalised in his poetry. Depending on the nature of the affair, the poems were sometimes bawdy, often dew-fresh and occasionally just so beautifully passionate that the lines are unforgettable.

In 1784, he flirted with Lizzie Paton, a rather coarse farm servant-girl, the result of which was his first illegitimate child. It was probable that Lizzie was merely available rather than attractive to Burns and in his poem, *My Girl, She's Airy,* he at first praises her slender figure but finishes with lines which are vulgar in the extreme. Lizzie Paton accepted that Burns would not marry her and disappeared from the scene, leaving the child to be reared by Burns' mother. However, Burns was proud of his sexual prowess in fathering Elizabeth and wrote in *A Poet's Welcome to his Love-begotten Daughter,*

> "Welcome, my bonie, sweet, wee dochter!
> Tho' ye come here a wee unsought for."

And in the last verse,

> "I'll never rue my trouble wi' thee
> The cost nor shame o't
> But be a loving father to thee,
> And brag the name o't."

He was always as good as his word.

During this time Robert met 18-year-old Jean Armour, the girl he eventually and rather reluctantly married, after she had given birth to their second set of twins. If he did not exactly keep her barefoot, he certainly kept her pregnant and in the kitchen. Meanwhile he lived his bachelor life, often being away for long spells to Edinburgh, where he was enthusiastically welcomed and entertained by a number of leading literary figures.

Married love did not usually inspire him. However at the height of his philandering in Edinburgh, he had a pang of conscience for his wife at home. The tender lines of *I Love my Jean* were set to the air of a strathspey,

> "There's wild woods grow, and rivers row,
> And money a hill between;
> But day and night my fancy flight
> Is ever wi' my Jean."

Poor, devoted, long-suffering Jean, she adored him, bore him nine children, the last one on the day of his funeral in July, 1796. She forgave his philandering and even took in his illegitimate daughter by barmaid Ann Park, only a few days after the birth of her own son, William. And to add insult to infidelity, he flaunted the affair in a poem which raised a few eyebrows in the genteel drawing rooms of Edinburgh.

> "Yestreen I had a pint o' wine,
> A place where body saw na;
> Yestreen lay on this breast o' mine
> The gouden locks of Anna."

If Robert ever truly loved any woman, it was Mary Campbell, the mysterious 'Highland Mary.' She was nursemaid to the son of Gavin Hamilton, Robert's friend and lawyer. His sexual adventure with her resulted in yet another illegitimate birth, but unfortunately, Mary and the baby died. She had been a welcome distraction for him at a time when he was in trouble with the Kirk Session and James Armour, over Jean's pregnancy and when he was considering getting away from it all by emigrating to Jamaica. It is possible that Mary Campbell had become his common-law wife and to marry Jean would have made him a bigamist.

In *Highland Lassie O,* he wrote,

> "She has my heart, she has my hand,
> By secret troth and honour's band.
> Til the mortal stroke shall lay me low
> I'm thine, my Highland lassie, O."

Certainly he had been totally besotted by her and his poetic muse knew no bounds. Amongst the many tributes to her is the hauntingly beautiful *Afton Water*.

> "Flow gently, sweet Afton, among thy green braes,
> Flow gently, I'll sing thee a song in thy praise;
> My Mary's asleep by thy murmuring stream,
> Flow gently, sweet Afton, disturb not her dreams."

Before his marriage to Jean in August 1788, Robert was in Edinburgh and once again apparently in a state of ecstatic love. The lady was Margaret Chalmers, to whom he wrote, "When I think I have met you, and have lived more of real life with you in eight days, than I can do with anybody else I meet in eight years."

But only a few weeks later, he was in love again, this time with Nancy McLerose, a married woman whose husband was in Jamaica. The lovers called themselves Clarinda and Sylvander and they wrote each other dozens of steamy letters. A more worldly-wise lady, she probably allowed him to love her at arm's length only and their passion was further hampered by his dislocated knee. He wrote for her, when she made the decision to join her husband, one of the finest love songs of all time, *Ae Fond Kiss*.

> "Had we never lov'd sae kindly,
> Had we never lov'd sae blindly'
> Never met – or never parted "
> We had ne'er been broken hearted.'

Lovesick or not, and with injured leg on a cushion or not, he managed to suspend his all consuming love for Nancy, in order to seduce Jenny Clow, her maid servant, no less. Once again, Robert had to record the affair in rhyme.

> "Oh Jenny's a weet, poor body,
> Jenny's seldom dry,
> She draigl't a' her petticoats,
> Comin thro' the rye!"

Poor Jenny, she paid dearly for her dalliance with Robert among the corn rigs. She became pregnant like all the others and lost her job. Robert, to his credit, did offer to take care of his illegitimate son (or rather Jean Armour would have taken care of him) but Jenny refused. She died of tuberculosis in early 1792. Another of his casual affairs in Edinburgh led to the pregnancy of a servant girl called May Cameron. There was no love poem for poor May, merely twelve shillings to persuade her to go back to the country and out of his life.

Yet Burns was till capable of composing the most delightfully innocent songs. Jean Cruickshank was the talented twelve-year-old daughter of a respected friend, and she and the poet enjoyed singing together at the harpsichord. For her, he wrote *A Rosebud by my Early Walk*.

> "Within the bush, her covert nest
> A little linnet fondly prest
> The dew sat chilly on her breast
> Sae early in the morning."

We do not know for whom *A Red, Red Rose* was written. This masterpiece is the most passionate poem of all. Perhaps every woman would like to think it was for her alone.

> "As fair art thou, my bonie lass,
> So deep in love am I,
> And I will love thee still, my dear,
> Till a' the seas gang dry."

All of Burns' love poems were not of equal merit, but the best are the finest lyrics in our language and were set to the most beautiful old Scottish melodies. For 200 years they have stirred the heart and reduced the listener to tears of genuine emotion. And they always will, for these songs are universal, they are the words of everyone in love, at all times and in every land.

But what about the poet himself? He belonged to an 18th century farming society where illegitimacy rates were high not only because contraception was unavailable, but also because it was considered a rite of passage in rural Scotland for young men to prove their manhood by seducing girls. He was never a reprobate although he was often a rascal. He was a genius who gave Scotland everlasting song, and this and all his other work will mark him as one of the greatest figures in world literature for ever.

But he was also a man… and a man's a man for a' that.

Robert Burns Said It First

(Published in the *Highlander*)

Good quotations help us remember the simple yet profound truths about life and can be stored in the mind ready for when we need comfort or inspiration. Only the Bible and the works of Shakespeare rival Robert Burns in meaningful, memorable lines, all of which come from his 559 published poems.

Contrary to some opinion, Burns was not an uneducated peasant farmer. As well as a poet he was also a prolific letter writer and all his letters were written in superbly constructed standard English and a large number of them are still in existence.

Although Burns did not attend school as regularly or as long as we do today, he had a firm grounding in English, mathematics and science and he even had a smattering of French. So he did not need to write in Scots. So why did he? The answer is simple. The Scots language was best suited to the sentiments he wishes to express and in spite of his work being in a dialect not always readily understood, his poems and in particular certain lines from his poems are known and quoted worldwide over 200 years after his death.

When we hear of an acquaintance not being able to follow a dream because of illness or adversity, we shake our head in sorrow and say, "Best laid schemes, poor man."

After Burns accidentally dug up the creature's nest with his plough leaving it unprotected in the winter, he wrote in *To a Mouse*,

"The best laid schemes o' mice and men
Gang aft agley
An leave us not but grief and pain
For promised joy."

"Of Mice and Men" which is a direct quote from the poem, was also the title given to the powerfully evocative novel by John Steinbeck, one of America's greatest writers.

In his poem *To a Louse,* Burns is sitting in church behind a rather grand lady who is unaware that a flea is crawling over her hat. Again these lines are world famous and so relevant to us all.

> "O wad some power the giftie gie us
> To see oursels as others see us.
> It wad frae monie a blunder free us
> And foolish notion."

Burns was able to acknowledge his own frailties and forgive those of others. In *An Address to the Unco Guid* he writes,

> "Then gently scan your brother man,
> Still gentler sister woman
> Tho' they may gang a kennin' wrang
> To step aside is human."

And equally relevant today, as these lines were in the 18th Century,

> "Man's inhumanity to man
> Makes countless thousands mourn."

The following amusing, tongue in cheek observation from *Tam o' Shanter* is much quoted at Burns Supper speeches,

> "Ah, gentle dames! It gars me greet
> To think how mony counsels sweet
> How mony lengthened sage advices
> The husband frae the wife despises."

But also in the same poem, we are reminded that life is short and we should enjoy it while we can.

> "But pleasures are like poppies spread
> You seize the flower, its bloom is shed
> Or like the snowfall in the river,
> A moment white, then melts for ever."

Burns's love poems in particular, show the Scots dialect being used to perfection. In such a store of memorable lines, it is difficult to select only a few. In *Green Grow the Rashes*, he confirms his appreciation of women.

> "Auld nature swears, the lovely dears
> Her noblest work she classes O
> Her prentice hand she tried on man
> And then she made the lassies O"

Every woman will agree that the following lines from *My Love is Like a Red Red Rose* are words to make the angels weep,

> "As fair thou art, my bonnie lass
> So deep in love am I
> And I will love thee still my dear
> Till a' the seas gang dry.
> Till a' the seas gang dry, my dear
> And the rocks melt wi' the sun
> And I will love thee still my dear
> While the sands o' life shall run."

Among dozens of his beautiful love poems, the following lines are particularly poignant and heart wrenching in their sentiment.

> "Ye banks and braes o' bonnie Doon
> How can ye bloom sae fresh and fair?
> How can ye chant, ye little birds
> And I sae weary, fou o' care."
> And from *Ae Fond Kiss,*
> "But to see her was to love her
> Love but her and love for ever."

and

> "Had we never loved sae kindly
> Had we never loved sae blindly
> Never met, or never parted
> We had ne'er been broken hearted."

Again in the masterpiece, *Tam O' Shanter,* Tam meets a group of ugly witches but there is one young witch who is very beautiful. She is wearing only a 'cutty sark' (a short undergarment) and Tam is enchanted with her dancing.

"And roars out, "Well done, Cutty Sark!"
And in an instant all was dark.
And scarcely had he Maggie rallied,
When out the hellish legion sallied.""

In the next century, *Cutty Sark* was the name given to the most famous tea clipper in the world, a sailing ship which was the epitome of the great age of sail. The vessel is now in dry dock in Greenwich, London and has captured the imagination of the millions who have visited her.

Perhaps aware that his own life would be short, in *The Selkirk Grace* Burns reminds us again that life is to be enjoyed. These impromptu lines were recited when he was asked to say grace before dinner, while on a visit to the Earl of Selkirk In 1794.

"Some hae meat and canna eat
And some wad eat that want it,
But we hae meat and we can eat,
And sae the Lord be thankit."

In 1795, a year before he died and already very ill, he wrote a prayer for the world in *A Man's a Man for a' That*. The poem has 40 lines but the last verse is optimistic for mankind.

"Then let us pray that come it may
(And come it will for a' that)
That Sense and Worth o'er a' the earth
Shall bear the gree an' a' that.
For a' that an a' that
It's coming yet for a' that
That man to man the world o'er
Shall brothers be for a' that."

Most people throughout the civilised world will recognise these three simple words, *Auld Lang Syne*. For some they will merely be words associated with Scotland. For others they will be part of a not very well understood piece sung at the end of a party or wedding when people join hands and remember the past and affirm the importance of the future and one's friends. But for some, it is an international expression of friendship celebrating the brotherhood of man. Here is the most famous chorus in the world,

"For auld lang syne, my dear
For auld lang syne.'
We'll tak a cup o' kindness yet,
For auld lang syne."

Robert G Ingersoll, the American attorney, humanist and powerful orator said about Burns, 'His name is dearer to a greater number of hearts than any other except Christ.'

This is a quote in which we, who have Scots blood in our veins, will find joy and comfort.

Maria Riddell

'The most Accomplished of Women and the Finest of Friends'
(Published in the *Leopard* and the *Highlander*)

Maria Riddell was young, beautiful, intelligent and witty and what was more, she also wrote good poetry. This woman, if circumstances had been different, could have been the love of his life, but instead, for two years, she became Robert Burns' kindred spirit and best friend.

From the time he moved to Dumfries in 1788, Burns had known her brother-in-law, Captain Robert Riddell, who had retired from the army. He lived with his wife, Elizabeth, at Friar's Carse, a neighbouring estate to the bard's farm at Ellisland, near Dumfries. The two men had much in common and in particular, Robert Riddell loved music and collected old tunes. He also had a host of influential friends and very soon, Burns had many new social contacts, including Robert's younger brother, Walter, and his wife Maria. At the age of sixteen, Maria Woodley had travelled out to the West Indies to stay with her father, the Governor of the Leeward Islands. There she met Walter Riddell and they were married when she was only eighteen. Later they returned to London before moving north to their new home in Dumfries. The house, which he renamed Woodley in Maria's honour, needed renovations, so meanwhile the couple, with their baby daughter, stayed at Friar's Carse during part of 1792.

Maria asked Burns to help her find a publisher for her book, *Voyages to Madeira and the Leeward Islands*. This work, illustrated with sketches of birds and animals, was based on a journal she had kept during her time in the West Indies. Burns wrote a very flattering letter of introduction for her to his own publisher, William Smellie, who had printed the Bard's Edinburgh Edition. The fifty-year-old publisher, who previously had little regard for young women and their scribblings, was completely bowled over by both Maria herself and the quality of her work. and he immediately arranged to have it published.

In a short time, Burns was enjoying the hospitality of both Riddell families. A great lover of drama and the smell of the greasepaint, he was delighted to join them in their box at the theatre. He was often invited for dinner at their houses and he and Maria began to exchange letters. They sent each other poetry for critical appreciation, and he borrowed books from the extensive library at Woodley. One of the more frivolous consequences of the war with France was the scarcity of French gloves for the fashionable ladies of Dumfries. However, Burns went to some lengths to track down a pair, which he sent with a note full of flowery sentiments. They also had serious discussions about health problems and the upbringing of their children. Maria kept all his letters, in chronological order, and they are available for posterity, but her correspondence to him vanished. Perhaps, after the death of Robert Burns, as a respectable married lady, she managed to retrieve her letters, which may have contained perceived indiscretions. Certainly Burns' letters to her showed a teasing friendship very close to love. This is also evident in the lines he wrote for her birthday when he imagines Winter complaining to the gods about having the worst weather of the year:

> "Now, Jove, for once be mighty civil;
> To counter-balance all this evil;
> Give me, and I've no more to say,
> Give me Maria's natal day!
> That brilliant gift will so enrich me,
> Spring, Summer, Autumn, cannot match me."

It is unlikely that Maria thought of Burns in the same way. Although Walter Riddell was often away in the West Indies, she had two young daughters and there is no evidence to suggest that her marriage was unhappy. Moreover, she was in a different social class and she was very sensitive to etiquette. She was also well aware of his reputation with women. But she would have enjoyed his flattery and attention and certainly, she admired his genius.

Then suddenly, it was all over. At the end of a convivial dinner party at Friar's Carse, the women had gone to the drawing room as usual and the men remained too long at the table drinking port. Someone had the idea that it would be fun to burst into the drawing room and do a re-enactment of the legendary rape of the Sabine women by the Romans. Unlike the historical event, this was only drunken horseplay, but Burns was the leader through the door whilst the others held back. It is likely that Elizabeth Riddell was the object of his amorous approach and the formidable, straight-laced lady was horrified and ordered him from the house.

The following morning, a very sober Burns was full of contrition and wrote a letter to Elizabeth. A simple, sincere apology might have worked, but Burns, failing to realise the gravity of the situation, penned a long, tongue-in-cheek piece of melodrama ending, "Regret! Remorse! Shame! Ye three hell-hounds that ever dog steps and bay at my heels, spare me! Spare me! Your humble slave."

Elizabeth did not forgive the 'humble slave' nor, surprisingly, did Robert Riddell, who had been his close friend for so long. Since her husband was out of the country, Maria was in no position to defend Burns, so the door of Friar's Carse was closed for him, permanently.

In the following weeks and months, he tried all kinds of excuse to re-establish his relationship with Maria. He returned books with flattering notes, he sent poems, but she did not respond. Eventually, the deep hurt at her rejection turned to anger and he began to behave like a petted child. He wrote five verses of uncalled-for attack on her, titled *Monody on a Lady Famed for her Caprice* and no one but himself could have been amused by his malicious little rhyme, *Lines Pinned on Maria's Carriage*.

> 'If you rattle along like your mistress's tongue
> Your speed will out-rival a dart:
> But, a fly for your load, you'll break down on the road,
> If your stuff be as rotten's her heart.'

A few weeks later, Robert Riddell died suddenly and Burns was distraught. The sonnet in praise of his estranged friend, which was published in the Dumfries Weekly Journal, did much to heal his wounded feelings.

Although etiquette did not allow them to meet, Burns and Maria did eventually start to correspond again. At first their letters were cautiously formal but soon they were lending books and sending poems as before. Once again he had someone with whom he could unburden his worries and express his frustrations without inhibition. He had much to worry about. His beloved daughter Elizabeth became very ill and died, he had financial problems and worst of all, his own health was deteriorating.

On July 7th 1796, Maria was in Brow, a little hamlet on the Solway Firth, recuperating from an illness. Burns was also there. On the advice of his doctor he was making a last desperate attempt at a cure by wading chest high in the freezing salt water of the Firth. The only good thing about being in Brow was that Maria was there and at last she felt it was appropriate to meet him again. She sent her carriage for him and they had dinner together. She was shocked at his condition and later wrote to a friend, "The stamp of death was impressed on his features." He was worried about his family and his wife, Jean, who was expecting their ninth child. He was also very concerned about how posterity would look on him.

This was their last meeting. Two weeks later, Scotland's Bard died at age thirty-seven, with Jean by his side.

Maria wrote a wonderful obituary, which was published in the Dumfries Journal. It was a sincere, warm-hearted account of his life and work. In it she forgave his frailties and paid tribute to his genius. It ended,

> "It is only on the gem we see the dust,
> The pebble may be soiled and we never regard it."

A Most Valued Friend

(Published in the *Leopard* and the *Highlander)*

Robert Burns regarded women primarily as potential bedfellows but there were exceptions.

One was the stunningly beautiful and talented Maria Riddell, with whom, if circumstances had been different, he might have enjoyed a marriage of true minds as well as bodies. But she was a respectable, upper class, married lady and out of his reach.

The other exception was Mrs Frances Dunlop of Dunlop, who was nearly thirty years older than Burns, physically unattractive and the mother of thirteen children. With her, he had a unique friendship, which, apart from five visits to her home, developed over ten years of written correspondence, of which 79 of Burn's letters and 107 of Mrs Dunlop's survive to this day. Posterity is indebted to this pen friendship, without which accurate knowledge of the life and times of our national bard would be much diminished.

In 1785, Mrs Dunlop's beloved husband of thirty-seven years died. In the same year, one of her sons, who had inherited Mrs Dunlop's childhood home, had to sell up in order to pay off gambling debts. The Wallace estate of Craigie in Ayr had belonged to her family for centuries and she was heartbroken. Later that year, a friend lent her a copy of Burns's first publication, the Kilmarnock edition of *Poems Chiefly in the Scottish Dialect.* She was especially delighted with *The Cotter's Saturday Night.* Mrs Dunlop was proud to be a direct descendent of Sir William Wallace, victor at the battle of Falkirk Bridge in 1298 and Scotland's national hero, so when she read the following lines, her depression lifted.

"O Thou! who poured the patriotic tide,
That streamed thro Wallace's undaunted heart.

Who dared to, nobly, stem tyrannic pride,
Or nobly die, the second glorious part."

Mrs Dunlop sent a letter to Burns at Mossgiel Farm 15 miles away, requesting six copies of his *Poems* and she also invited him to visit her at Dunlop House. Burns replied that he would be delighted to send the five copies remaining but that he was about to go off to Edinburgh to organise a further edition.

This was the beginning of a close friendship lasting ten years and when it ended, both of them were very hurt.

Her letters to him were always very long and rambling, written in a cramped, almost undecipherable hand. It would have required a determined effort to read to the end of them. His letters to her, unlike his poems, were always in perfectly constructed Standard English. In his first one, he established their relationship by praising Wallace in exaggerated flowery terms.

So Mrs Dunlop moved into his life. He sent her his newly composed poems; she took on the self-imposed job of literary advisor attempting to 'improve' his verse and persuading him to remove vulgar passages to make it more socially acceptable. She read *The Twa Dogs*,

"Then sat they down upon their arse,
And there began a lang digression
About the lords o' the creation."

She wanted him to replace the offending word with "tails." He didn't do this but in a later version, the line was changed to,

"Upon a knowe, they sat them down."

She was always pointing out trivial faults but, depending on his mood, he either ignored her advice or rejected it with good humour.

She also tried to discourage his use of the Scottish language in his poems. Thankfully, Burns rejected this advice also. His very best work, *Tam o' Shanter, Holy Willie's Prayer, To a Mouse, The Twa Dogs*, and many others including his love songs are in the Scottish language, which was the perfect medium for the sentiments he wished to express. However, after the triumph of the Edinburgh Edition, which gave him national acclaim, he was confident and arrogant enough to write to Mrs Dunlop,

"Your criticisms, Madam, I understand very well, and could have wished to please you better. You are right in your guess that I am not very amenable to counsel. Poets, much my superiors, have so flattered those who possessed the adventitious qualities of wealth and power that I am determined to flatter no created being, either in prose or verse, so help me God!"

However, only the mediocre are at their best all the time and later, he admitted to some work that he was not overly proud of.

Mrs Dunlop also took the role of the caring, sometimes scolding mother of a genius child. As their friendship deepened, she knew when he was troubled and usually succeeded in getting him to talk about it. She knew and disapproved of his sexual affairs. We know more about his affair with 'Highland Mary' from his correspondence with Mrs Dunlop than any other source, yet he says very little about Agnes McLehose, for whom *Ae Fond Kiss* was written. When he married Jean Armour, he wrote, attempting to explain why he had failed to choose a more appropriate wife, "'Circumstanced as I am, I could never have got a female partner for life who could have entered into my favourite studies, relished my favourite authors, without entailing on me, at the same time, expensive living, fantastic caprice, apish affectation, with all the other Boarding school acquirements."

This and several other remarks about Jean before and after his marriage suggest that his love for Jean was not all-consuming. His second legitimate son was named Francis Wallace Burns in honour of his friend. He wrote to Mrs Dunlop again, "About two hours ago, I welcomed home your little Godson. He is a fine squalling fellow with a pipe that makes the room ring. His mother as usual. Zelucco I have not thoroughly read so as to give a critique on it." The four words between the joy at his newborn child and an opinion on a novel show a coldness towards the woman who was his loyal, devoted and long suffering wife.

Knowing that his poetry and attempts at farming were not enough to support his growing family, Mrs Dunlop sent his children gifts of money and she also set about trying to get him a better paid job. Eventually after failing to persuade him to join the army or take a lectureship at Edinburgh University, she gave up and he secured his post in the Excise Service by other means, but she was always ready to put in a good word for him any time it was required.

Their friendship cooled a little in 1791. Mrs Dunlop's milkmaid, Jenny Little, was a prolific though very average rhymer, but her mistress persevered in trying to get Burns to critique her poems. Burns was not interested and ignored every effort Mrs Dunlop made to push the girl's efforts under his nose. One day, however, the determined milkmaid turned up at Ellisland clutching her poems. Unfortunately her timing was disastrous. Jean was about to give birth, the house was in disarray and Burns arrived home with a broken arm having fallen off his horse. This was hardly an appropriate time for a poetry reading and Jenny had to leave, bitterly disappointed. Strangely, Mrs Dunlop's sympathies lay with her maid. She paid for the girl's book of poems to be published and upbraided Burns for his haughty dismissal of it.

Their relationship survived this episode but in 1794 it deteriorated quickly and finally. Two of Mrs Dunlop's daughters were married to French aristocrat émigrés; Britain was now at war with France and four of her sons had army connections. But Burns continued to be a fervent supporter of the French revolution and his politics were in complete opposition to hers. After receiving a particularly insensitive letter about liberty and the gallant people of the Revolution, she stopped writing to him. He was bewildered and hurt at her stony silence and in his second last letter to her at the end of January 1796, he begged her to communicate with him again. He wrote despairingly about the death of his beloved only daughter Elizabeth and his own worsening illness, but still Mrs Dunlop did not relent.

Two weeks before his death he wrote farewell letters to several people including Mrs Dunlop. He said, "Your friendship which for many years you honoured me was a friendship dearest to my soul. Your conversation and especially your correspondence were at once highly entertaining and instructive. With what pleasure did I used to break up the seal! The remembrance yet adds one pulse to my poor palpitating heart. Farewell!"

Although the letter was lost or destroyed, probably by Dr James Currie, who was the first biographer of the poet, he did confirm that Mrs Dunlop had indeed replied and that the last letter that Burns was able to read on his deathbed contained the longed for words of reconciliation, from his old most valued friend.

Reply to the Toast to the Lassies

(Montrose Bowling Club Burns Supper)
(without the help of any notes!)

Thank you, Eddie, for your kind words about the lassies (well, they were mostly kind words, I think) and thank you, Andy, for asking me to reply.... even if you did say that it didn't matter if it was good or bad as long as it was short. It was more important, you said, to get on with the dancing!

Also in a letter to his friend, Robert Maxwell, in 1789, Burns wrote "I have ever observed that when once people who have nothing to say, have fairly set out, they know not when to stop." ...So I've got the message.

So all I'm going to do is say a little about marriage, then and now. Rabbie finally married Jean Armour (very reluctantly) in 1788. From 1786 to when he died in July 1796, Jean had nine children (although not all of them survived,) so it was true to say that if he didn't exactly keep her barefoot, she was always pregnant and in the kitchen. Her last son was born on the day of his funeral. Also in the house was the daughter Rabbie had by Lizzie Paton in 1785, and Jean's generosity of heart extended to mothering his love child (or maybe lust child) by Anna Parks born at the same time as her own son, William. Apparently she merely sighed and said, "Our Rabbie should have had twa wives."

We don't know how much she knew about Mary Campbell (Highland Mary,) who is thought now to have died giving birth to his child. He was very secretive and sentimental about her and it is just possible that he loved her. She is the subject of one of his loveliest poems:

114

"Flow gently, sweet Afton, among thy green braes
Flow gently, I'll sing thee a song in thy praise
My Mary's asleep by thy murmuring stream
Flow gently, sweet Afton, disturb not her dream."

Then when he was off on his celebratory visit to Edinburgh, he met Nancy McLehose, with whom he had an affair…mostly, it is thought, by steamy love letters. She was a sophisticated married lady, whose husband was in Jamaica. She couldn't risk an unwanted pregnancy, so she probably kept him at arm's length. Again one of the loveliest poems of all time is for her, *Ae Fond Kiss.* At this time he had a dislocated knee but this, and his all consuming passion for Nancy, didn't stop him from seducing her maidservant, Jenny Clow. Poor Jenny paid dearly for her poem, *Comin' Through the Rye.* She became pregnant (like all the others) and lost her job. Rabbie, to his credit, did offer to take care of his illegitimate son (or rather, have Jean take care of him,) but she refused and she died not long afterwards of TB. About the same time he had a casual acquaintance with a barmaid called May Cameron. She of course also became pregnant but poor soul, she didn't even get a poem…
..only ten shillings to get out of town and out of his life.

And that's only the tip of the iceberg. Absence never made the heart grow fonder for Rabbie. When one girl was unavailable, he always consoled himself by the appearance of another. And many were immortalised with a poem. It was uncertain which girl some poems were dedicated to.

Apparently Annie Rankine, the daughter of a local farmer claimed,

"Corn riggs and barley riggs
An corn riggs are bonnie O
I'll ne're forget the happy night
Amang the riggs wi Annie O"

After his death, another *five* Annies in the district claimed the poem!

The long-suffering 'stand-by-your-man" Jean must have known what was going on…at least some of the time. She's bound to have had just a wee clue when he read her his latest poem, titled *My Bonnie Mary*.

Yet she was devoted to him. After he died, she describes the day when he composed *Tam o' Shanter*. It was summer and she herself was stuck in the kitchen making cheese and trachled by her children. She watched him from her open kitchen window. He was striding up and down, totally inspired, talking to himself and laughing uproariously at his own lines; she knew with great pride that this was going to be a masterpiece.

She was a woman of practical good sense and in her widowhood her maturity and dignity impressed everyone who met her. And her surviving children were a credit to her.

In its way, her marriage worked because the burden of a successful marriage lies with the woman. No woman today would put up with Rabbie's behaviour. But women then had no choice. They made their bed and they had to lie in it. Today, we have the upper hand; we have our men far more under control, better trained and their actions far more closely scrutinised. But we're not there yet, girls. There are still a few loose ends to be tidied up. Husbands should never, for example, be allowed to buy their own clothes, there should be a nationally agreed upper limit for their pocket money (maybe £10 a week?) and football on television should be banned. I would go as far as banning all football, especially that World Cup and European Cup nonsense, which fills their wee brains every so often….and speaking of football brings me neatly to our sport….bowls. Think carefully about this, ladies, do we really want a so called equal partnership in bowls?…Because, like marriage, we would end up taking full responsibility for it…and, also like marriage, they'd enjoy the best bits and then sit back and let us worry about all the rest. And why would they do that?…because, ladies, like Rabbie, they are MEN…..and a final quote from the man himself,

"And for a' that , an a' that, a man's ONLY a man …for a' that."

(thunderous applause??)

Eight

Women's Short Stories

Computers, Roller Blades and Old Fashioned Love

(published in *My Weekly*)

A ndy McLeod's mum said that it was best to be young, single and fancy free but Andy wasn't so sure if he agreed….not if single meant standing with the lads at the school dance pretending to be enjoying himself….and fancy free meant that he couldn't even day dream. No, Andy was quite sure that he wanted to be in love. What he wasn't so sure about was whether the girl of his dreams even existed and if she did,….well, what would she think about him?

Aged seventeen and a half, Andy stood six feet, three inches in his socks. In spite of large platefuls of stovies, double helpings of bread and butter pudding and a milk bill which made Jenny McLeod flinch, Andy was a beanpole. With size 14 shoes and hands like spades, he was painfully aware that he was hardly every girl's idea of a hunky male. But his worst feature, he considered, was his mousy brown hair, with the vertical tuft at the crown which refused to lie down, in spite of much combing and liberal applications of his mum's hair lacquer.

Not that the female sex didn't like him. On the contrary. Little three year-old charmers engaged him in earnest conversation in supermarket queues and his granny and her chums bought him shortbread at coffee morning cake and candy stalls.

All his female classmates liked him, especially Charlotte. She kept getting error messages on her computer like 'illegal operation,' or 'system failure.' Most recently, she had phoned, "Andy, I haven't pressed any funny keys, honest, at least I don't think I have, but the wee grey box on the screen says, 'invalid V x D dynamic link call' and Dad is in the middle of doing the farm accounts. Could you be a darling again, please!" To Charlotte, Andy was a knight in shining armour....well, at least a knight who rushed to her aid on shining roller blades and who knew all there was to know about temperamental computers. But Charlotte was a petite five foot redhead and Andy knew that she wasn't the Miss Absolutely Perfect from his day dreams.

Andy's problem was that, at the moment, he didn't have a social life. He seldom went out in the evenings as he was studying for his pre-university exams and besides, he had his early morning paper round.

Now, at seventeen and a half, Andy considered himself too old to be a paper boy. But after four years, getting up at 6.30am every day of the week except Sunday had become a habit, and anyway, he needed the money....shoes for someone with size 14 feet did not come cheap.

To be honest, Andy enjoyed his paper round, which took him forty-five minutes on his roller blades. He started at Prospect Terrace and this was where a black scruffy dog of unidentifiable breed always appeared from the back lane. Fred chased after the roller blades round the empty streets and pavements and guarded them closely when Andy disappeared in his socks into the entrance of the big block of flats in Melville Row.

The very last house on his round was Daisy Carter's bungalow in Balmoral Avenue. Daisy was a farmer's widow, a spritely, keen-eyed lady who had always been an early to bed, early to rise person and at the age of seventy-four, did not intend to change the habit of a lifetime. Every morning she was at her door at 7.25 waiting for her Courier, which she took pride in reading from start to finish, including both the quick and cryptic crosswords, before nine o'clock.

One January morning when the sleet was blowing horizontally down the street, she had taken pity on her shivering paper boy and invited Andy into her kitchen for toast and jam and a mug of tea. This would have been a one-off occasion if Fred hadn't decided that two digestive biscuits and a bowl of water were just what a tired dog needed at the end of a paper round. So the following morning, with an exceeding lack of good manners, he squeezed past Daisy into the kitchen and stood looking meaningfully at the biscuit tin.

So, for over three years, Daisy Carter entertained her two friends between 7.25 and 7.35 almost precisely. Andy gossiped about school, football and computers, and lately, his woeful lack of success on the girl front.

Daisy once said to Andy, rather wistfully, "I would love to have a computer. I suppose I would be too old to learn, wouldn't I?" A few months later, after several Sunday morning tuition sessions, Andy's septuagenarian pupil was sending poems to women's magazine with some considerable success and astounding the members of the Ladies Bowling Committee with her immaculately produced minutes and competition lists. She was even talking about going on to the Internet, e-mailing her son in Australia and banking on line. "The rate of interest for EGG is much better than conventional banking" she informed Andy, who for once didn't know that.

Then one frosty morning in early November, Andy and Fred had just left Daisy a minute or two later than usual, (Andy had been changing the colour cartridge in her printer) when he met THE GIRL. Actually if it hadn't been for some fancy footwork with his roller blades, they would have collided head on. He recognised her immediately as Miss Absolutely Perfect from his dreams, a blue eyed blonde haired beauty, five foot eleven inches of sheer gorgeousness wearing a navy track suit and white trainers.

"Sorry!" she said.

"Sorry!" he said, blushed and whisked off his unfashionable woolly hat knitted by his granny for the cold mornings.

She glanced at the rogue tuft of hair which wouldn't lie down, grinned at him, ran on the spot for two seconds, then jogged on, her blonde pony tail swinging rhythmically from side to side. As Andy stared after her slim figure, heavenly bells rang in his head, a forty piece orchestra played Wagner and his heart rate shot up to 150 beats per minute. "Wow!" he said to Fred, "Wow...eeee!"

After that, Andy always arranged to leave Daisy just as the girl jogged past. But after twenty-seven magical mornings, not a lot had really happened. Andy's heart always danced a reel when he saw her, he wore a perpetual grin on his face and his Mum worried about his loss of appetite.

Their conversations, however, continued to be brief.

"Hi!" he said on nine occasions.

"Hi!" she said, also on nine occasions.

"I'm Andy McLeod," he said on the tenth morning.

"Hi, Andy!" she said on day eleven.

"Vanessa James, eighteen in May," she volunteered the next day.

"He's Fred!" on day thirteen.

"Hi, Andy! Good morning, Fred!" She bent and fondled the dog's ears and rubbed the white patch on his chest. Fred sat there, loving it, his tongue hanging out and his eyes closed. Andy almost felt jealous.

From then on, Fred ran to the end of the street to meet her. By the time she reached Andy she was jogging again.

"Hi, Vanessa!"

"Hi, Andy! Bye, Freddy boy!" And that was it. Every day they greeted each other and Andy just roller bladed back to the shop and Vanessa just ran on.

On day twenty-seven Fred accompanied her.

"Well, thanks a million," muttered Andy to Fred's departing tail. "Some friend you are!"

He consulted Daisy about how to get to the next stage, how to start a conversation, how to get to know her. But Daisy shook her head and said that life hadn't been quite so complicated fifty years ago when she met her Jim at a farmers' ball.

A week later, Andy's stomach lurched in horror as he roller-bladed to a halt at Daisy's house. There was no light in the kitchen and the front door wasn't open. He felt physically sick with fear. Something was obviously wrong with Daisy. He banged on the door and Fred barked. He shouted through the letter box but there was no response.

In his panic, he didn't even notice at first that Vanessa had joined him. Afterwards Andy noted happily that not only was Vanessa the most beautiful girl in the world, but she was also level-headed, practical and the kindest, sweetest person. She quickly discovered that a neighbour had a spare key and within a few minutes Andy was bounding up the stairs to Daisy's bedroom.

He and Vanessa were greatly relieved to see the old lady stir and emerge slowly from beneath her duvet. "Oh dear" she said weakly, "Have I slept in? I've been surfing, I think I must have been surfing until about half past three."

"Oh, you poor darling," said Vanessa, taking her hand. "Andy, we'll need to phone the doctor, the poor soul's been suffering for half the night. Has the pain gone now?"

"No, no," said Daisy, now looking her usual chirpy self, "Surfing, my dear, surfing the Internet. Once I boot in, I simply forget about the time. I'm fine, really I am."

After tea, toast and jam and digestive biscuits for Fred, Daisy, still in her dressing gown, waved goodbye to her young friends. Vanessa was jogging slowly and Andy was roller-blading slowly. She couldn't quite see but she thought they were holding hands. Fred was dancing first at Andy's side, then at Vanessa's.

Daisy watched them until they were out of sight. With a little secret smile of satisfaction she poured herself another cup of tea and sat down to do the crosswords.

Valentine Girl

(Published in *My Weekly* in February 1999)

"Look," I said with mock severity to my class of fifteen-year-olds, "Do you think we can forget about Valentine cards just for an hour and get some work done?....No, Tommy, nobody sent me one."

"Not even Mr Gardener?" said Billy with a grin, and the class laughed. One Saturday morning I had met my colleague in the local library. Instead of school talk, we exchanged authors and ended up in the coffee shop in the High Street....a careless thing to do in a small town. By Monday morning, half the school knew about it.

"Okay, you lot," laughing with them, "Let's get on with the second most important thing in your lives....trigonometry. Yesterday we found a formula to deal with the triangle when it is not right-angled...."

Later I walked round the classroom, helping and checking and Angie, truculent, scowling-faced Angie, looked up from her maths and beamed at me.

"I got one," she whispered and produced a large pink envelope covered in glitter pen hearts, from inside the cover of her jotter. The class was silent. When anything is whispered in a classroom every ear is out in stalks.

"Oh, nice," I attempt to say nonchalantly. "But maths now, Angie, please."....but I smiled and patted her on the shoulder.

Three days before, on the second Saturday in February, I had one of my low days. The sleet was throwing itself horizontally against the window and I remembered it had been a similarly stormy day when Alan died almost exactly a year before. The family were coming to be with me on Sunday, but on that dreary Saturday I couldn't settle. It was too stormy even to take the car out of the garage. The rugby international appealed only slightly more than the horse racing and old movies on the other channels. I chose a selection of my favourite CD's and in a flash of inspiration, I decided to tidy out the drawer in the kitchen. Everything that had no other place ended up in this drawer, odd buttons, bits of string, supermarket money-off coupons long out of date, and keys which didn't fit any known lock.

I pulled out the drawer and laid it down on the carpet in front of the fire. Tucked into the instruction book for the cordless phone, I found the Valentine card. I remembered buying it to give to Alan, knowing it would be the last one. But in his final desperately ill days, Alan was long past caring that his wife of thirty-five years might send him a Valentine card. So it was never written and never delivered.

Alone in my quiet living room I indulged once again in the tears that were never far away and I took his photograph from the mantelpiece and studied it for a few moments. I held the card out to the flames, hesitated for a moment and then withdrew it.

Suddenly I thought of Angie, angry, rebellious Angela, who had problems too heavy for her young shoulders. As her guidance teacher as well as her maths teacher, I saw more of Angie than any of my other pupils. Our relationship had almost developed into one of exasperated parent and impossible daughter, but I had grown fond of her and I wanted very much for things to go right in her life. Mr Stewart was an alcoholic who often humiliated her by appearing drunk at the school gates. Her mother, unable to cope, sometimes left the family home for days at a time and Angie made herself responsible for her thirteen-year old sister, Debbie.

Often life just got too much for Angie. She never handed in homework, she lost books and played truant. Teachers got the backlash of her frustration and I spent many a lunch hour just listening to her problems and providing a shoulder to cry on.

"Tomorrow there will be something else for everybody to talk about," I attempted to console her on the last occasion her father had to be escorted from the school grounds. "It's not where you have come from, it's where you are going," and I would launch into my usual speech about the importance of education and how well Angela could do if she put her mind to it.

But my exhortations always fell on deaf ears and it had been a hard year for her and for me.

And so an idea flickered through my brain. "I wonder," I said to myself, and I phoned my granddaughter.

"Claire, darling, would you do something for me? When you come down with Mum and Dad tomorrow, bring your fancy glitter pens….and you would know some Valentine rhymes, wouldn't you? No, it doesn't matter if some of them are a bit rude….and no, of course not, I'm not sending it to Brian Gardener. Who told you about him anyway?"

Amazing, the news of my coffee had obviously reached the family, ten miles away.

"I'll tell you all about it tomorrow. See you about mid-morning. Bye, sweetheart."

So the lovely card on which I had originally intended to write a simple message of love for my dying husband was transferred into a piece of teenage fun. Claire covered every square inch with rhymes and hearts and kisses. She gave the envelope similar treatment after I had dictated the address.

From the hilarity coming from the loft, we guessed that Neil and Kate had discovered the box of old family photos. Afterwards we all watched the replay of the rugby match. Neil said how thrilled his dad would have been to see Scotland's resounding victory and we cried a little and hugged each other.

But when I went to bed that night I thanked God that the first anniversary of Alan's death had not been as bad as I had dreaded and I slept better than I had done for months.

Angela came charging into my classroom after school dinners, as usual, without knocking. I was eating a sandwich as I marked homework. She was still smiling as she handed me the card.

"Beautiful, isn't it?" she asked, pushing aside the jotters and easing herself on to my desk.

"This rhyme is a bit rude, isn't it? And whoever he is he spells love, LUV." I pretended to inspect the card in typical teacher fashion. "Who do you think sent it?"

"It was George. I sort of guessed it might be him. I always thought, well....hoped that he liked me. So I caught up with him in the corridor after maths and I thanked him for it. He's utterly gorgeous!"

"Who's George?" I asked, genuinely puzzled.

"George Graham, of course, silly. Sorry, Mrs Clark, but you know George. He sits at the back beside Jimmy."

I smiled at the picture of the quiet, studious beanpole that she described as gorgeous George.

"What did he say? I asked.

"Well he *said* he didn't send it, but he would, wouldn't he? You should have seen him. He was blushing to the roots of his hair....and anyway, Debbie says his wee sister has a whole set of these glitter pens." Her pale face was pink with excitement. "And guess what, he came and sat down beside me at the dinner table. He says he'll meet me in the library and help me with my maths homework."

"Angela Stewart, you are quite capable of doing your own maths! And besides, when was the last time you bothered to hand in any homework?"

"I know, I know," she grinned at me. She swung her legs and contemplated her Doc Marten boots. "But maybe it's time for a change. He *is* drop dead gorgeous, isn't he, Mrs Clark?"

Before I could reply, Brian Gardener knocked and put his head round the door.

"Oh, sorry,....hi, Angie." And to me he said, "Are you remembering to give me a lift at four? They said my car should be ready about half past."

Angie slid off the desk. "Come on in, Mr Gardener. I'm just off to the library."

"The library?" teased Brian, "The Angie we all know and love going to the library?"

She held her head high. "Mr Gardener, my name is not Angie, it's Angela. And yes, the library. If you really want to know, I'm meeting my boyfriend at half past one."

She picked up the card from my desk and put it in her bag carefully. She beamed at both of us. "So I'll just leave you two on your own to discuss cars....or whatever else you teachers get to talk about."

New Love on a Friday Afternoon.

I finish off the school week with 3S, my favourite class of six boys and two girls. Yes, only eight pupils, and they say that teachers are always complaining about overwork.

Already Jimmy and Dale are niggling each other and I do my single handed United Nations Peace-Keeping Force routine. My small class of fifteen-year-olds have all the problems of the typical teenager. Moody, tired, hyperactive, depressed, they can be all that. Like other youngsters their confidence is skin deep, literally. A couple of acne spots on the chin and their world falls apart.

But my pupils in 3S have other problems, problems too heavy for their young shoulders. Their confidential files reveal epilepsy, dyslexia, abuse, abnormal family arrangements and a desperate lack of grey cells. I love them all dearly and I think they like me too....with that indulgent fondness they would have for a dotty old grandmother. Fine, maybe I can multiply 75 times 24 in my head, but who else on this planet has never heard of ARCTIC MONKEYS or thinks that OASIS is a green patch in the desert with palm trees?

They have spent the last hour at cooking, making shortbread, most of which they have consumed coming along the corridor. But they have left some for me. Their gifts are laid out on my desk wrapped in paper towels or toilet tissue.

We start, as usual, with our mental arithmetic. Two weeks ago, they impressed the inspector with their ability to calculate in their heads, sale discounts of 10%. And Dale, who normally has the concentration span of an exhausted amoeba, explained to the inspector that if the total at the supermarket was £4.03, it was a good idea to offer 3p along with the note to save the change in the till. At the end of the lesson, Dale was singled out for special praise and he has been smug ever since.

But they are unable to continue for long and get easily bored and I spend considerable time and ingenuity preparing work for them. On a Friday afternoon, when their brains have almost shut down for the weekend, the Maths has to be heavily disguised.

I tell them to look at the old nursery rhyme I have written on the board.

> MONDAY'S child is fair of face,
> TUESDAY'S child is full of grace
> WEDNESDAY'S child is full of song
> THURSDAY'S child is brave and strong
> FRIDAY'S child is loving and giving
> SATURDAY'S child finds joy in living
> But the child that is born on the SEVENTH DAY
> Will have great success along life's highway.

I have adapted the original version. Well, what Wednesday's child wants to be told he is full of woe? And as for Sunday's child being good and gay! Heaven forbid!

They protest that this is a Maths class, poems are for English and nursery rhymes are for babies. 'Trust me, you'll enjoy this,' I assure them and ignoring further complaints, I settle them and we carefully discuss the meaning of each line. They are getting interested. Jimmy says that his Mum told him he was born on half day closing. 'You're probably right,' I agree with a sigh. 'That's why you are so fond of music,' and he does yet another impromptu drum roll on his desk with two pencils.

I glance at Davie who, as usual, is sitting apart from the others, hunched and silent, at his desk at the back of the classroom where on this dreich winter afternoon, the fluorescent light doesn't reach.

As always he has his head down and his face expressionless. Davie is a six-foot beanpole but he does his very best to be invisible. Even his writing is so small and cramped that I cannot read it. I wish I knew what to do about Davie.

I show the class a method of calculating the day when you know the date of birth. It involves dividing by 4, adding, then dividing by 7 to find a remainder which will correspond to the days of the week. I explain it slowly and carefully and we confirm that Jimmy was, as he thought, born on a Wednesday. They are eager to get going and I go round the room helping and checking.

At last, they all finish their calculations. Debbie Cook is Monday and I declare (and my look defies anyone to contradict me) that Debbie is indeed very beautiful. Gracie-Jane Gourlay says she's Friday. Five feet, ten inches and fourteen stone of sheer good nature, yes, that's G-J. Connor is Thursday and the others agree that the boy in 3B who had been teasing their classmate about his skinny frame deserved his thumping. Unless he was completely stupid, he wouldn't bother Connor again, they said.

In the gloom at the back of the classroom I see Davie lift his head. He coughs and flushes deeply. For the first time in eighteen months I think he is going to say something. He looks over at me, then at Gracie-Jane. 'I'm Tuesday!' he blurts out, 'I'm Tuesday!' I am puzzled and so is everybody else....except Gracie-Jane who gets the message immediately. With a big grin on her face, she rises from her seat, gathers up her belongings and with size 9 high platform shoes stomping across the room, she strides over and sits down next to Davie.

I suggest to the class that they repeat the exercise for another member of their family and I sit down at my desk to observe what is going on at the back. I'm witnessing a miracle. I'm seeing a new Davie. Gracie-Jane is smiling and feeding him pieces of shortbread and he is blushing and grinning broadly. I say, 'Excuse me, Posh and Becks, get on with your work, please!' but the severity of my words is softened by my smile. They look at me, eyes shining, then they look at each other. They giggle and move closer together, as they pretend to restart their calculations. The others make kissing noises and the class is in danger of getting out of control.

But the bell rings for the end of the school week. I dismiss the class and they start towards the door.

'Have a nice weekend,' they shout.

'Don't do anything I wouldn't do!' Dale says to me and they all laugh.

Gracie-Jane and Davie are in the midst of them, still whispering to each other. Davie is walking tall and straight and he has a look of happy confidence. I am so proud of him.

It is one minute after four and the school has that empty silence of a world after a nuclear explosion. I brush shortbread crumbs off Davie's desk, pick up my briefcase and switch off the lights. My usual Friday afternoon weariness has gone and I feel foolishly happy.

Hot Gossip

(published in *My Weekly* January, 2008)

No one dares to phone me during *Coronation Street* except foreign gentlemen announcing that I have won a world cruise in a competition I haven't even entered.

It was Rosalind, also known as Nosey Rosie by the other inhabitants in the lane. "Kate," she said, "Are you remembering that tomorrow there will be no garden refuse collection?" Unfortunately, of all people, Rosalind and her sister had been sitting two tables away from Tom and me in the cafeteria in the afternoon. She wouldn't have been able to hear any of our conversation in spite of her ears waggling like satellite dishes in a hurricane but curiosity was obviously getting the better of her.

"You know me, Kate, I never pry, I am not that sort of person, but I was just wondering who….."

"Thanks for reminding me about the green bin, Rosalind," I interrupted, "Please excuse me, my sauce is boiling over," and I hung up.

Five minutes later, the phone rang again. It was Gemma, my granddaughter, so I reluctantly turned down the sound. She never starts with "Were you golfing today, Gran?" or "Is your hay fever any better?" Gemma always gets straight to the point. "I'm doing my geography project on the computer," she said. "And it's got to be in by tomorrow morning. I need to make a table for recording temperatures."

I resisted the urge to tell her that it was Wednesday at 7.45pm and anyway, the homework should not have been left to the last minute. But I love my granddaughter dearly. She and I are the best of pals and if she needs my help, that definitely comes before the never-ending problems of the Platt family. I am proud to be the acknowledged computer expert in our family, but Gemma is no novice either. "Just click on the window shaped icon which says *Insert Table*," I said whilst attempting to lip read the dialogue on the TV screen at the same time. "That was easy," I accused her. "You've been able to do that for years."

"Er...probably," she said vaguely. There was obviously something else on her mind. She hesitated, then added, "By the way, Emma's mum saw you in the supermarket cafeteria this afternoon with a man. So....who was that, Gran?"

When I didn't respond immediately, she said, "Come on, Gran, fair's fair, I told you about Jamie." She lowered her voice and whispered, "Have you got a boyfriend too?"

"Don't be ridiculous, Gemma!" I laughed. "He's someone I occasionally see on the golf course. He just happened to be in the coffee queue the same time as me."

"Hmm, OK, if you say so," said Gemma doubtfully. "Nobody I need to tell Mum and Dad about, then?"

"Of course not, darling," I said, "Now get your homework finished and leave me in peace to see the last few minutes of my favourite soap."

******

My daughter phoned twenty minutes later. By this time *Coronation Street* had changed to a programme about silicone breast implants. Like her daughter, Claire got straight to the point. "Mum, who is the male friend you were having coffee with this afternoon?"

I was trying hard not to look at the TV screen but I stared with horrified fascination at a woman with long blonde hair and huge lips the colour of blackcurrant jelly who was proudly displaying a bust for which no cup size has yet been invented.

"Mum! Are you listening?" Claire said.

"For goodness sake," I said, "Tom Stewart was behind me in the coffee queue. I didn't have my reading glasses and I pushed the

133

button for milky coffee instead of black. Well, Tom offered to take the milky one and, because the place was very busy, we sat down at the same table. There, that's it, now you know all the boring details! .... By the way, what are your new neighbours like?"

Claire ignored my attempt to change the subject. "I know him! He used to have the South Gate Garage, didn't he? That's where Dad used to have his car serviced....in fact, he's Angela's Dad.... remember she was at school with me? She emigrated to Australia when she got married. We still keep in touch occasionally."

I knew all this already but I said, "Really? Is that so?"

The TV programme had moved on to liposuction. A large lady was having her spare fat sucked out with a vacuum cleaner. For a moment or two, I considered this as an alternative to giving up chocolate biscuits, but Claire was saying, "Mum, are you going to see him again?"

"Claire," I said in exasperation, "I see him most Tuesdays and Thursdays on the golf course. He plays with his pals and I play with Maggie, Sybil and Jean. We will wave to them across the fairways as usual....and no, before you ask, we did not make a date to have another exciting rendezvous in Tesco's."

"Hmm," said Claire in exactly the same tone as her daughter. "Thanks for helping Gemma with her homework. It's not like her to leave it to the last minute.... Guess what? We think she's got a boyfriend."

I didn't say that I had already heard all about the wonderful Jamie, best footballer in the school, with his 'cool' spiky blonde haircut and his 'cool' taste in music. Instead I replied, "Has she? Well, no doubt she'll tell you about him when she's ready." I smiled as I hung up.

What I hadn't mentioned to Claire was that Tom and I chatted for almost two hours. Although I didn't get round to asking him if he watched *Coronation Street* we covered a lot of ground. We discussed the problems of cooking for one, our addiction to crosswords, how our gardens were doing, the beauty of recent sunsets and the progress of our mutual golfing hero, Tiger Woods. We were also amused by the gorgeous baby who sat in his high chair at the next table, a happy smiling little chap who wanted to share his soggy biscuit with us.

****

Maggie phoned at quarter to nine. One of those 'how to sell your house and get as much for it as possible' programmes was on. The poor couple finding it difficult to sell their property were being scolded for treating their house like a home. A house, we were informed, is an investment. What buyers are looking for, apparently, are bare floor boards everywhere, all furniture and decor beige or white, and a kitchen with floor to ceiling stainless steel and more electronic gadgets than Star Ship Enterprise. Also there must be no evidence of the occupants having hobbies like knitting or reading the Sunday newspapers. However, I am not planning to move so no camp young designers are likely to faint with the sheer horror of seeing my pale cream carpeted bathroom or flowery chintz curtains. I sighed and pressed the OFF button on the remote control.

"Kate!" said Maggie, "What's this about you and Tom Stewart? Sybil saw you in Tesco's when she went in to do her weekly shop. She said you were both still in deep conversation when she was at the check-out. Is there something you're not telling me?"

"Maggie," I said wearily, "There's nothing to tell….honestly. We met by chance, had a coffee. Full stop."

"OK, darling," said Maggie, "But if I ever need to buy a posh hat, you will give me plenty of warning, won't you?"

"Maggie McDonald!" I exploded. "You are my best friend, but sometimes you are outrageous!" However, we were both laughing as we hung up.

****

The following morning the phone rang again. My heart skipped a little beat when he said, "Hi, Kate, Tom here." I could tell he was smiling. "If I'd known how much gossip there would be over one cup of coffee, I would have suggested the all-day full English breakfast and a jam doughnut to follow," he said.

I laughed. "I take it you've been getting interested enquiries too?"

"You would not believe this. Angela phoned from Perth….Perth, Australia, that is, and said she had heard the news. What news? E-mails must have been flying through cyberspace non-stop all night."

He hesitated for a moment. "I don't suppose you would fancy trying out the new Italian restaurant on Saturday? It's had very good reports."

"It will also be very busy," I warned. "With spies everywhere. There will be more gossip."

"With a bit of luck, someone will discover that your one woman neighbourhood watch, Nosey Rosie, has a secret live-in lover half her age and that will divert attention," Tom said.

I never giggle but that's what I did. "OK, we'll count on that happening, then. Thanks, Tom, I'd love to have dinner with you."

"Great, I'll book it and get back to you…. by the way, I've a confession to make…. I don't like milky coffee either."

Nine

Poetry

Blue Tit Spring

(This poem won first prize in the AWC annual poetry
competition.)

In Spring, when the blue tits come
and choose my garden to bring new life,
I'll remember Lorraine
who shared my delight.

Last year I wept.
Though they came again,
she was no longer here
to watch these perfect birds
perform the miracle of birth.

Nor was there joy in planting things.
But yet, Spring flowers pushed their frosty heads
above the frozen earth.
Their beauty thawed my ice-bound heart.

This year, the little birds are back
and from the blue tit box
new birds will fly.
And my soul will shine,
for I know that life goes on
and nothing really dies
but just takes comfort from the earth
and rests its head.

Ten

Letters

19 Bents Road,
Montrose,
Angus.

28 November, 1994

The Manager,
Rose Street Restaurant,
Jenners,
Princes Street,
Edinburgh.

Dear Sir/Madam,

On Saturday, 26 November, about 1pm, laden with bags of Christmas shopping in the correct shade of dark blue with gold lettering, my friend and I took time out to have a large filled roll and a coffee in the Rose Street restaurant.

My friend found a table while I collected the knives and teaspoons. Knives? What knifes? Several people were hovering round the cutlery bar, juggling trays and parcels, viewing the empty knife section.

In a not unreasonable tone, I asked a wee assistant if she would go to the kitchen for the missing cutlery. Some time later she reappeared with the news that all the knives were in the dishwashing machine. One of the diners suggested that just this once, she could wash a few by hand. She disappeared once again but re-emerged to announce that hand washing wasn't allowed nor could she deliver the knives to our table when eventually the dishwasher had done its job.

So with our coffee now lukewarm we set about tackling our filled rolls without cutlery. Two ladies at the next table were skilfully

140

spreading butter and jam on their scones with the wrong end of their teaspoons.

But the ham and other fixings slipped out of our roll, down our chins and on to the plate and that's not very ladylike for two retired schoolteachers, is it? My granddaughter tells me that you never get cutlery when you buy a Big Mac, but ladies who lunch at Jenners do expect a little more refinement.

A few minutes later, I went hunting for knives once again. One gentleman waved a knife in the air. "I've got one," he smirked like one who had just won the National Lottery. Sadly, however, the knives had disappeared again, like snow off the Calton Hill in August.

My friend and I will be back at Jenners for the January sales. Will you have enough knives then, do you think? Or perhaps you will allow a small discount if we bring our own.

Yours faithfully,

Elizabeth Strachan.

PS This letter prompted a very amusing reply in "Prime of Miss Jean Brodie" style with a £20 voucher for the restaurant.

Letter to the Editor

(Published in the *Montrose Review* in November 1992, after an exiled Montrosian, Donald Kirkwood, dared to write to the Editor and state that present-day teachers
weren't a patch on those who taught him several decades before. This prompted a deluge of angry replies from both teachers and parents.

Rose Coloured View of Happy? Schooldays.

Sir,

I refer to the paragraph in Guest Gable Ender where Mr Kirkwood reminisces about schooldays forty years ago.

Surely you are looking through rose-coloured spectacles, Mr Kirkwood. In the stifled atmosphere of rote learning, abstract methods and discipline by terror, many children were under-achievers.

In today's modern classrooms, our youngsters are encouraged to discuss, investigate and learn in practical situations. No one is made to feel stupid for asking questions and admitting that they do not understand. If there is a peaceful hush in the classroom, it is because everyone is engrossed in what they are doing, not because some tyrant is standing at the front with a belt.

In the "good old days," children were seen and not heard and they were expected to be deferential to those in authority, whether they deserved the respect or not. But society has changed and the methods of yesteryear's teachers would now be inappropriate and even ridiculous.

Come and see us at work, Mr Kirkwood. Many fine young people leave Montrose Academy. Perhaps you will agree that we deserve some of the credit.

So in reply to your question, "Are there any teacher now half as good?" I would say, Yes, Twice as good!

Yours etc

ELIZABETH STRACHAN
Senior Teacher
Montrose Academy

Letter to the Editor (2)

(In reply to an article by an entomologist claiming that wasps are harmless)

Sir,

Entomologist George Else, of the Natural History Museum in London, was quoted (Press & Journal 7 August, 1991,) as saying "Most wasps sting only if provoked and mostly those who are stung, quite frankly, are asking for it."

Who is this deluded hymenopteranophile? Everybody knows that wasps have the well-deserved reputation of Count Dracula. Has Mr Else never made jam and gone into mortal combat with dozens of these stripy stingers who intend to sample your Rasps '91 or die? Has he never taught in a classroom where the disruption caused by the kamikaze swoops of only one wasp kills a lesson stone dead?

Our family call these bad tempered insects "wapses" after our tiny granddaughter used to call imperiously from her pram, "Wipe the wapse, Grandad," with a feeling for alliteration way beyond her years.

These friendly wasps that Mr Else loves must surely be dead ones, entombed behind glass in his Natural Museum.

Yours etc

ELIZABETH STRACHAN

Letter to the Editor (3)

(A letter to the editor of the Saga magazine, published May 2002)

Who is the person, the clever, devious person with a twisted mind, who compiles the Saga Prize Crossword? I have to admit to a mild crossword addiction and I attempt several in a week, including the *Times* and the *Sunday Times*, but the *Saga* crossword is by far the most difficult and makes no allowances whatsoever for the ageing brains of the *Saga Magazine* readers.

This month (May), it was particularly difficult and I almost abandoned it but I struggled on and, once again, I have successfully completed it.

What a lovely feeling of satisfaction it gives me to send it off. Maybe now I'll have time to get my housework and gardening done.

ELIZABETH STRACHAN

Eleven

Children's Stories

Sparkle and the Garden Birds

(written for my twin granddaughters)

The birds sit high in the apple tree,
And Sparkle purrs on Ellie's knee.
She strokes his fur. He loves all that.
"Who's my sweetest darling cat?"

But Sparkle is a cunning cat.
When Ellie's gone, he's just a brat.
The ball of fluff she loves to hug,
Is a bird-chasing, nasty thug.

Blackbird is the first to say,
"Your Royal Whiteness, if I may,
With your permission, Sir, come down,
And pull that fat worm from the ground.
I do love worms, they're so delicious.
Quite like spaghetti, but more nutritious."

"Listen, Blackie, and listen good,
Don't search my garden for your food.
Don't come again, 'cos if you ever,
I'll munch you to the last black feather.
And!... your baby birds... their nest's not hidden.
It's in MY hedge...and that's forbidden."

On the table, there's a shortbread crumb,
And Robin says, "Sir Fluffy Bum,
Please may I have that tasty treat,
I never have enough to eat."

"You cheeky bird, it's Ellie's cake,
You can't have that…for heaven's sake!
And if you're hungry, I don't care,"
He gives poor Rob an angry glare.

Bluetit hangs on the coconut shell.
"Your Gorgeous Softness, you look well!
I think you're stunning! Indeed I do!
May I help myself to a peck or two?"

"Look, small Bluey, let's get this straight,
I rule this place from house to gate.
I don't care what *you* think of me,
You're just a bird in the apple tree.
But in this garden, I'm the King,
So you can't have nuts…or anything."

The starlings soar in the clear blue sky.
They see the cat, so down they fly.
"Fat cat Sparkle, we don't like you-oo,"
And they splatter him with birdie-poo!

Other birds join in the game.
They tease the cat and call his name.
"Poo-ey Sparkle," sing all the crows,
And big fat tears run down his nose.

"You wicked birds! Just look at me!
My fur's a mess. Oh, I can see,
I'll need a bath and I hate that.
I'm a poor, dirty, sad old cat."

The cat hides under the garden seat,
So all the birds fly down to eat,
The yummy nuts, the squishy worms,
The crunchy seeds, the tasty crumbs.

They sing and dance on the washing line.
They've had a feast. They feel just fine.
But poor old Sparkle's very smelly,
He meows and meows and cries for Ellie.
Ellie comes. She hears him cry.
"My Precious Pet, my Sweetie-Pie,
These birds are bad to my darling cat."
She cleans his fur. He's pleased with that.

Now Sparkle purrs on Ellie's knee,
And the birds all laugh in the apple tree.

Daisy's Wishes

(Winner of the 2007 SAW competition for a children's short story)

Daisy was bored. The other cows were happy to spend all day eating the sweet green grass and lying in the shade of the oak tree discussing the handsome bull in the next field, but Daisy wanted something different.

One morning, as she returned from the milking shed, she noticed the ponies galloping round the paddock. "I wish I had long slim legs like that," said Daisy. "I could prance and dance in the sun all day long."

The Farmyard Fairy was seldom busy. Sometimes in the Spring, a sheep would wish to have two baby lambs instead of only one, and sometimes a hen wished to lay an extra egg, but, really, she had very little to do. Mostly she just sat on the gate, looking pretty in her straw hat, pink dungarees and little pink wellies.

The Fairy heard Daisy's wish and was delighted to help. She waved her magic wand and chanted,

> "I'm the Farmhouse Fairy and Daisy begs
> For me to give her pony's legs."

And to the horror of all her friends, the cow's legs grew long and thin as sticks. Daisy was very pleased with her lovely legs although she was far too fat to manage even a tiny gallop.

An eagle was soaring and gliding in the clear blue sky, her tawny brown wings glinting like gold in the sunshine.

"That's what I should have wished for," thought Daisy, "How wonderful it would be to fly."

The Fairy was sure she could do better this time and waved her wand really hard, saying,

"Farmyard Fairies can do most things
So let's give Daisy eagle's wings."

In a flash, beautiful feathers sprouted on Daisy's back. But Daisy was too heavy to fly. Once, when the wind blew strong, she rose up in the air, but fell back on the ground again with a thump. The other cows laughed at her. They said cows were not meant to have huge golden wings and skinny legs. "You look absolutely stupid, Daisy," they said and turned their backs on her.

One evening, when all the cows were settling down to sleep, Daisy heard a nightingale singing in the starry sky. "I wish I had a voice like that," sighed Daisy, "They wouldn't laugh at me if I could sing."

The Farmyard Fairy wanted to get her spell just right this time and waved her wand extra hard.

"Our Daisy wishes one more thing
Now she wants the power to sing."

Daisy stood up on her slender legs, spread her huge wings and opened her mouth. She sang all the latest pop songs, and *Old Macdonald had a Farm* twenty-three times. No one at the farm got any sleep that night and in the morning all the animals were tired and grumpy. On the way to the milking shed Daisy tottered behind on her skinny legs. "Wait! Wait for me!" she cried in a high sing-song voice, but they ignored her.

After a few days, Daisy grew sad and lonely because she had no friends like herself. She wasn't a proper cow and she wasn't a pony or an eagle or a nightingale.

The farmer was angry. "Daisy is no longer one of my prize winning herd of dairy cows," he said. "She's a sort of NIGHTING-PONY-EAGLE-COW-GALE. We'll have to put her in a zoo."

"Oh dear, oh dear," cried Daisy. "I don't want to go into a zoo. I've heard some of the animals in there are not very friendly. I wish I were a cow again."

The Farmyard Fairy said, "Look, Daisy, I'm very sorry but I have many other things to do now. The farmer is wishing for rain to make his potatoes grow and the children are wishing for the school holidays to be warm and sunny. So I am too busy to be bothered with you." But then she looked at Daisy's lovely cow face and the big brown eyes brimming with tears.

"Okay, Daisy," she said, I'll give you one last wish."

Once again, she chanted a spell,

> "Isn't it lucky that I know how
> To turn this creature back to a cow."

The other cows watched as the long slim legs and the magnificent wings disappeared. They ran to meet her and she mooed and mooed with sheer joy.

Daisy lived happily ever after, eating the sweet green grass and giggling with her friends when they spied the handsome bull in the next field.

Twelve

Funny Stories

Alarming Elsie

A s Elsie joined the back of the queue in the home bakery, a girl touched her on the shoulder. "Excuse me, madam, but I think you have taken something from our shop which you haven't paid for."

"Me? What are you talking about? What shop?...I've just come in to get the new health loaf with sunflower seeds. I haven't even been served yet," said Elsie.

"Not this shop. You have been in *Modern Lady*, madam, and you have set off the alarm. I would be obliged if you would come back to the store with me." The girl took her arm firmly.

Elsie Macdonald, retired headmistress of North Park Primary School, had never broken the law in her life. She had never exceeded the speed limit, nor had a parking fine. She had never dropped litter ....she had never even been overdue with her library books.

The assistant led Elsie along the High Street and as they crossed the threshold of the brand new store, the alarm sounded.

"Please come over to the counter with me, madam," said the girl and spoke into her phone, "Miss Burton required at the front checkout immediately."

"Look," said Elsie, "I did come in ....only for a minute.... to see this lovely new store, but I didn't buy anything."

The girl ignored her. A grim-faced woman wearing a black suit approached them. The label on her lapel said 'T. Burton, Manager.'

"Would you mind emptying your bag, madam?" she said, and Elsie turned out her Harrods shopper, which she had bought with her sister, Jean, at Gatwick airport. Out tumbled half a pound of

Barclay the Butcher's best steak mince, the *Radio Times*, a piece of filleted haddock for Sparkle, who refused to eat cat food, and her purse.

"My sincere apologies, madam, it's obvious that you have taken nothing from our store and the security cameras confirm that you were here for only fifty seconds and touched nothing. However, something is setting off the security alarm. I think it's probably your shoes."

"It couldn't be these old things," said Elsie, taking them off and handing them to the assistant. "These shoes have been through airport security and into almost every shop in the town and they have never ever set off any alarm."

However the assistant rubbed the soles of the shoes on a pad on the counter. "There you are! The shoes are now de-activated. There shouldn't be a problem again," said the manager.

She walked with Elsie to the door and the alarm went off. Elsie jumped hurriedly back into the shop. "What on earth could it be?" she said, but she wasn't worried now, only curious. It would be something really interesting to tell her bridge club friends in the afternoon.

"Goodness only knows….new system…. maybe ultra sensitive…. I'll have to report it to Head Office, but please feel free to shop any time at *Modern Lady*," pleaded the manager. "If you'd like to come back to the counter, I'll be delighted to give you a £10 voucher to compensate for all the anxiety and embarrassment you've had."

The ladies at the bridge club were intrigued. Usually they stifled yawns when Elsie pontificated about modern education and how standards had deteriorated since her long career as head of North Park School. She was now the centre of attention and the ladies laughed and joked about visiting her in prison and smuggling in her cat. There were a few aces trumped that afternoon, but no one noticed.

Next morning, Jean phoned. "I've been thinking," she said, "Did you have that new shopper with you, the one covered with pictures of cats, which we bought at the airport? Let's go up to the High Street and you can stand outside on the pavement. I'll take the bag into the shop and I bet the alarm'll go off."

"Well, I walked out of Harrods with it, not to mention all the places I've been with it since and there has never been the slightest peep from any alarm. But, okay, we'll give it a try," sighed Elsie.

Jean walked in and out of the store with the bag and then in and out again but there was complete silence. "Well," she said, "That means it must be something in or maybe....**on** your body." Jean eyed her sister's trim, but curvy figure with suspicion. "Is there something you're not telling me?"

Indeed Elsie did have a secret, one she didn't intend to share with anybody, not even her sister. She didn't mind being five feet, four inches and a very slim seven stones but she had always hated her flat chest. Before she retired, she used to stuff lamb's-wool into her 34 AA cup bra, which gave her a little bit of shape, especially in the summer when she had to abandon her chunky knit cardigans. However, the lamb's-wool made her itch and often she needed to lock the door of her office while she gave herself a long, blissful, satisfying scratch. And once, she remembered with horror, she had reached up to the top of a wall map and her pretend bosoms shot upwards and sat on her shoulders. When she retired, she threw out everything along with the shapeless cardigans and resigned herself to a pancake flat old age.

Then, a few weeks before the incident at *Modern Lady,* she was in the dentist's waiting room when an advert in a magazine caught her eye. 'For a soft and natural shape that adapts to your body contours, Glamora adhesive breast forms will never slip or move and are particularly suitable for ladies with sensitive skin. £220 for two. Beautiful black lace bra worth £20 free with orders before 1st October. All sizes available,' it said.

Elsie rather admired the ample bosoms of the actresses in these celebrity magazines but she knew that anything larger than a modest size 2 would set tongues wagging in the bridge club. However she sent for size 3 and they were everything the advert claimed and more. She loved them.

But Elsie's problem at *Modern Lady* continued to puzzle her until one morning she woke up with the answer. She looked at the box which held her breast forms overnight. 'Made in China,' she read. '65% silicone, 35% other materials.' She looked up 'silicone' in the dictionary which said, 'A class of polymers with a chemical structure of alternate silicon and oxygen atoms.'—"Whatever that means, Sparkle," said Elsie to her cat.

She waited until the next rainy day and returned to the store, this time flat-chested. With her raincoat hood almost covering her face, she stood just inside the threshold shaking out her umbrella. As she'd suspected, the alarm did not go off.

From that day on, she never went out shopping without her gorgeous new bosoms. She visited her favourite store often because they sold such pretty things and with her lovely figure, everything she tried on looked good.

'Sexy,' was not a word that had ever been applied to describe Elsie Macdonald. Indeed, she herself classified it as a swear word, never to be uttered. She abhorred its use in magazines as the obligatory adjective for everything from perfumes, male celebrities badly in need of a shave, to ridiculous modern furniture. But when she tried on these crisp cotton shirts with, of course, the top two buttons undone, her image in the cubicle mirror, if not the 's' word, was definitely rather attractive.

"We'll be asking you to model for us one of these days," said Miss Burton. When she paid at the checkout, the assistants were friendly and often walked with her to the door. They shook their heads sympathetically as the 65% silicone (or maybe it was the 35% 'other materials') activated the security alarm once again.

Just before Christmas, Elsie was in a fitting room at *Modern Lady* trying to decide which of three tops she would buy to wear at the bridge club dinner. At the other side of the curtain, she could hear two of the assistants talking.

"That old dear who always sets off our alarm, I'll bet she was a real battleaxe of a headmistress," said the younger one.

"Head Office think that it may be some kind of metal in her false teeth that is activating our sensitive new security system," her colleague was saying. "She may be a silly, harmless old bat now but I still wouldn't dare ask her to remove her dentures!"

Elsie did the unthinkable. She stuffed the pearl encrusted cashmere sweater in her shopper.

But the assistants were still discussing her. "To be fair," said the second woman, "She was a terrific headmistress, she just lived for her school. She loved the kids and they loved and respected her. Do you know Jimmy Peters? You know, Peters' Garage on the North Park Industrial Estate? Well, he may be a very successful man now but when he was a wee lad, there were real problems at home and he often didn't turn up for school. Miss MacDonald told him the janitor needed someone reliable to ring the school bell in the morning and at playtime and after dinner. Given this important job, Jimmy never missed a day at school again. Yes," the assistant said as they moved away from the area of the cubicles, "Jimmy and many others have a lot to thank Miss Macdonald for."

Elsie felt the tears well in her eyes. She took the sweater from her shopper and put it carefully back on the hanger. She returned it and the cream silk blouse to the rail, paid for the red sequined top and walked to the door. As usual, the alarm bell sounded and she waved to the shop assistants.

"It's okay, it's only me," she laughed, and they waved back.

tryatrio.com

(unpublished)

The travellers, who heaved an enormous trunk and two suitcases into the boot of the old Volvo and squeezed another two large bags on to the back seats, were not as Callum and Maggie expected.

Leo had not aged well. He was even smaller than Maggie remembered from their university days and she couldn't decide if the orange colour of his thin face was caused by advanced liver disease or an over application of some cheap fake tan. The knees of his jeans were missing and his open sandals revealed very dirty feet.

Leo had said on the phone that his girlfriend, whom he had met in Vladivostok, was an athlete and Callum had imagined her, slim, dainty with hair in girly ribbons. But Svetlana was not, and never had been, a teenage gymnast. Her tracksuit trousers were several sizes too small and her grubby plunge-neck T-shirt revealed enormous bosoms, for which no bra had yet been invented. Her black hair was scraped tightly back from her pudding face which glowered at them during the introductions. "I vant to go now!" she demanded. "I vait too long at ziss airport. I vish to go to bed." She pushed Maggie aside and sat in the front passenger seat.

There was little conversation on the journey to the flat because, hidden behind the two bags, Leo had fallen asleep and Maggie was speechless with fury.

Callum attempted to break the silence. "What is your particular sport?" he asked.

Svetlana wound down the window and stuck a foot out. "I am...

how you say?...all round at ze sport."

"You can say that again!" muttered Maggie from the back seat.

As usual, the lift was out of order, so Callum, Leo and Maggie struggled up the four flights of stairs to the flat with the trunk, two cases and a bag. Svetlana followed them with the smallest item, cursing in Russian.

The luggage was deposited in the spare bedroom, and immediately Svetlana lifted Leo, swung him round, like an Olympic hammer, onto the bed and closed the door.

Callum attempted to placate Maggie. "Look, it's only for a few days, for goodness sake. It's not his fault that his money hasn't been transferred from Russia."

"But what exactly does he do for a living?" asked Maggie. "We always thought that he did some hush-hush job for the Foreign Office, but now he says he's here to read his poetry at the Fringe. He's like an ageing hippy backpacker." She laughed, "He must think we're a right couple of staid old bores in staid old boring jobs. Well, I suppose, if it's only for a couple of days..."

For two weeks, Leo assured Callum of the imminent arrival of his money. But every evening Maggie came home from school to find the guests still there, sometimes in bed, sometimes consuming vast quantities of food and vodka on the table where Callum was attempting to work on his computer. Occasionally Leo scribbled in his notebook and the poem he produced was hailed by Svetlana as a masterpiece. "Who's Svetlana's clever leetle boy, zen," she growled and, in grave danger of being suffocated in the folds of her enormous breasts, Leo was carried off to the bedroom.

At the beginning of the third week, Maggie returned home after a very trying day with Class 5, to find that Svetlana had been practising her discus throwing skills by spinning her fat body like a top and hurling dinner plates out of the kitchen window. Callum and Leo had taken refuge in the public library all day fearing they might suffer the same fate.

"They'd better be gone by tomorrow," warned Maggie. "YOU brought them here. YOU get rid of them."

Callum concocted a story about Charlotte, a name he had always liked. Charlotte, he explained, was a close friend of Maggie who had walked out on her unfaithful partner and was in urgent need of a room.

In the end they went readily enough, especially when Callum slipped Leo five £20 notes to cover their first few days in a B&B. Unfortunately, they insisted on taking only one suitcase, promising to collect the rest of their luggage when they were settled.

Three peaceful days later, Callum spotted them outside. "Good God!" he thought, "I'll need to convince them that Charlotte is still here." He grabbed two T-shirts and a pair of jeans out of the laundry basket and flung them on the bed, along with his own pyjama top and a copy of *Penthouse* (confiscated by Maggie from one of her class of nine-year olds.)

Leo had returned to collect his notebooks. "I intend to sell some of my poems to the *Times* and the *Scotsman*," he said. "I expect that will bring in a hundred or two."

Svetlana was inspecting the garments on the bed. "Ziss slut, she vear no knickers," she observed.

"Ah, well," said Callum, "She is a very sexy lady."

Leo looked up from his notebooks. "Is she really?" he said.

Over the next month, Leo and Svetlana returned to the flat several times for items from their luggage and each time, Charlotte's room looked more lived in. Callum and Maggie often slept in the bed to make it authentically crumpled and they sprayed the room with expensive *Joy* by Jean Patou. Maggie bought black lace stockings and draped them over the dressing table mirror and a copy of *Lady Chatterley's Lover* (another confiscation from Class 5) lay open on the pillow.

Callum told a very interested Leo that Charlotte was a bisexual psychologist, a natural blonde, tall and slim with very long legs. She was highly intelligent and very sexy. He and Maggie were very fond of her.

"Ziss tart Carlotta, she read ze dirty books," said Svetlana.

"No, no!" said Maggie, who had never actually read the book

but had noticed the blurb on the back cover. "It's a classic which explores previously unchartered areas of human experience in post First World War England."

"Humph!" snorted Svetlana, "Ees Eengleesh sheet!"

In early November, Leo arrived alone at the flat to collect another suitcase. His poems had been returned by both newspapers and his money was still missing. He looked at Callum hopefully but getting no response, he said, "I must meet Charlotte. She'll be back from work soon, so I'll wait."

For four seconds, Callum's face froze in blind panic but then he relaxed as a brilliant idea popped into his head. "Er, no, you can't do that, old pal. Not at the moment. It's all too new. Besides, you've pinched every girl I've ever had except Maggie."

Leo smirked, but it was only partly true. In their university days, when Leo was all teeth, tan and tight trousers, some of Callum's more petite cast offs were quite happy to be passed on to the diminutive Romeo. But, Callum thought, if all Leo could get now was the fat, foul mouthed, pseudo-athlete from Vladivostok, he would be better off celibate.

"What d'ya mean, too new? What's too new?" demanded Leo.

Callum hung his head in an attempt at shyness. "Well...we're having a trio...Charlotte, Maggie and me."

"Wow!" said Leo, "You lucky devil! I wonder if Svetlana would fancy that. I doubt it, though.... not enough room in the bed for one thing....and I know it's hard to believe, but not everyone likes Svetlana." His satsuma-coloured face looked crestfallen for a moment, then his eyes lit up. "I feel a poem coming on. Yes, I'm definitely feeling a sonnet...yes, trio... mio...Leo... Charlotte?... not even a poet of my calibre could get anything to rhyme with that...never mind...I'll call her Lotty, so we have naughty, haughty, little botty...oh yes, I'm a genius."

Abandoning the suitcase, he dashed down the stairs, two at a time.

Maggie was enthusiastic about Callum's idea. After all, it was only an imaginary trio. She was still Callum's wife and soulmate who wore white cotton Sloggies and greyish over-washed bras, but now she also got to be Charlotte who wore satin lace thongs, black leather skirts twenty inches long and pink jewelled sandals with four inch heels. She felt completely different when she dressed as Charlotte, more intelligent, more confident and certainly much sexier. One day, she went to school as Charlotte and the class was stunned into open-mouthed silence the whole day. Callum and Maggie now preferred to sleep in Charlotte's bed every night, where they enjoyed reading each other excerpts from *Lady Chatterley's Lover*. Maggie was intrigued with the character of Connie and she thought the scandalous love affair with Oliver Mellows was very exciting. She began researching the fashions from the 1920's and other periods of history. Her mum, who was a dab hand with a sewing machine, ran up a few authentic looking garments and didn't ask any awkward questions.

Callum had another idea. He designed a new website and called it 'tryatrio.com' and very soon he was getting hundreds of hits in a day. For only £3 (€ 4.20 or $6), Maggie offered a download of the on-line magazine of the same name. Worldwide, there were over 8000 downloads in two days. In the first edition, readers particularly liked the article *Love Your Trio? Try a Quadro,* so Maggie followed it up in the second edition (this time there were more than 12000 downloads) with *Can You Handle a Quintro?* E-mails, stories, requests to advertise and items for the problem page came flooding in. Meanwhile, Maggie's mum was busy making copies of the garments worn by famous literary characters throughout the ages, including Antony and Cleopatra, Romeo and Juliet, Napoleon and Josephine. She even had to employ two assistants.

In the third edition, Callum advertised a special offer in musical vibrators. For only £40, or their equivalent in euros or dollars, there were three to choose from. The *1812 Overture* by Tchaikovsky was available for the enthusiast but, surprisingly, it was outsold by *The Flight of the Bumble Bee* by Rimskij-Korsakov. However, the most popular one by far was the one which came in a tartan box and played *Donald Whar's Yet Troosers* by Andy Stewart. The money rolled in and although Maggie and Charlotte vehemently disapproved of sex toys, they said, "Callum, darling, business is business."

In mid-January, Leo and Svetlana discovered again that the lift to the flat was not working. Carrying a suitcase, Svetlana heaved and puffed her way up the four flights and with each step, she repeated her favourite expletive…the one that uses every letter in the Russian alphabet. She was in a particularly bad mood because the Immigration Department had got wind of her whereabouts at the B&B.

Leo had been fantasizing about Charlotte for weeks and he clutched a large notebook to his chest. He had decided to be firm with Callum. "I'm going to insist on seeing Charlotte," he said, "I know she'll just love my poem."

Svetlana spat. "Poem ees sheet, Carlotta ees sheet, a-a-all is sheet. Anyvay, ze tart must go, ve need to haff back ze room."

Their luggage was piled on the top landing with a note taped on the trunk. Svetlana fingered it suspiciously. "Fat ees theese? Fer am dem bastards?"

Leo read, "Hi, you two. Belated good wishes for the New Year. As you can see, we are no longer here. The flat was getting overcrowded but luckily we are now much better off and we've moved to a new pad in Morningside. You may be able to contact us at our website, tryatrio.com.

Good luck,

Callum, Maggie, Charlotte, Lady Constance Chatterley, Oliver Mellows, Sir Lancelot and Lady Guinevere, Rhett Butler and Scarlett O'Hara."

The Christmas Adjudication

(written for the AWC Christmas party)

When the president introduced him as 'J. Trumperton-Smythe, best-selling novelist,' James felt once again that little frisson of pride.

James used to be Jimmy Smith, who worked in the Co-op and in his spare time wrote stories of romance in faraway places. The miracle happened when he read somewhere about the power of a good sounding name; which prompted him to send his first novel *Katmandu Kisses,* by J Trumperton-Smythe, to Mills and Boone. They accepted immediately and asked for more.

He stood up and removed his leather jacket to reveal tight faded jeans and a crumpled black shirt with the top four buttons undone.

"I am delighted to judge your Christmas prose competition," James said, smoothing his pony-tail, "But disappointed there were only seven entries. No matter, I enjoyed reading all of them. I'll say a little about each piece—in no particular order—then, at the end, I'll announce the winner.

"The first one is 'Decorating Your Cludgie for Christmas,' and it's by Flush, who describes how to get the 'smallest room' ready for the festive season."

James enjoyed matching a story with its author, but this time, no one in the room looked mad enough to paint Santa and his reindeer on a toilet seat and scatter the floor with artificial snow.

"This next one," he continued, "Is called *Love in the Library* by Milly. A nice man meets a nice lady in the library and they have a nice chat about the possibility of a white Christmas. He asks her to go for a coffee...which is nice...but later on she sees him with a beautiful girl...which isn't so nice. Well, guess what? It's his sister...so everything turns out nicely in the end. Yes, a lovely feel-good story, so well done, Milly."

He looked around the room and decided *Love in the Library* belonged to the old lady in the corner who was smiling at him.

"This next story, *Sailing to Happiness,* by Mermaid, is about a lonely woman who finds romance on a Christmas cruise to the Antarctic. Beautifully written, it does, however, have a few confused clichés. For example, 'The captain was the handsomest man since sliced bread,' isn't *quite* right and 'Penelope swept the deck with her dark eyelashes,' conjures up an unfortunate picture."

James looked round the room again. A white-haired man was writing notes but the old lady in the corner was still beaming at him.

"This next piece, *Christmas Love,* by Rhymer, doesn't quite fit the genre being as it is, a poem. However, I'll read the first of the ten verses.

> Oh, how I long to be
> Under the fairy-lit Xmas tree
> Where you and I will sip our tea
> And you will say that you love me."

"Bloody Hell," said the man with the flashing bow tie, "That's Archie's old poem... again. He's always doing it...changing the tree to suit the competition. Last time, it was called *Desert Love* and they sat under a stupid waving palm tree."

"Well," retorted Archie, "My wife says it's the best poem she's ever read."

Someone near the door muttered, "It's probably the *only* poem she's ever read."

Sensing trouble, James moved swiftly on to the next story. "I cried all the way through *Requiem for Billy,* by Tweety Pie. The sadness at the death of the author's budgie on Christmas morning is relieved only a little by Billy's colourful vocabulary. That little bird knew every swear word in the book!"

168

No one in the room looked like a bird fancier except, perhaps, the old lady in the corner.

James picked up about 150 single spaced pages. "I've had to disqualify this entry as I suspect it has more than the maximum 1000 words," he laughed. "Its title is *Some Day My Prince Will Come* by Princess. Chantelle, a keen golfer, watches a celebrity match at Carnoustie. Tiger Woods and Prince Andrew are playing down the eighteenth fairway when a wayward shot strikes Chantelle on the head. The Prince rushes over to apologise. Their eyes meet. It is love at first sight. But there are many obstacles to be overcome before Chantelle finally gets an invitation to join the royal family for Christmas at Sandringham. I am confident that this story would make a wonderful women's magazine serial."

The author revealed herself immediately, by bursting into loud sobs. Her friend patted her arm and others muttered their congratulations.

"Now, for the last one," said James. "*The Office Party,* by Sexpot, is not so much a story as four steaming pages of literary Viagra. The employees of Snodgrass Ltd celebrate their Christmas bonus by drinking gallons of booze and performing a multiple christening of the mahogany boardroom table. I wish I could write sex scenes like that," he sighed.

He knew who Sexpot was.

"Well, it's a tough decision, but the winner is…" He paused for maximum dramatic effect.

"Bloody well get on with it!" grumbled Archie.

"Okay," said James. "The winner is…" Another long pause. Archie groaned. "*The Office Party*! Now who is Sexpot?"

He turned to the blonde woman on his left with the plunging neckline revealing a very attractive bosom. She ignored him and collected *Requiem for Billy.*

The old lady in the corner jumped up, waved her arms in the air, wiggled her skinny hips and sang, "Sexpot, Sexpot, I'm your lovin'…. Sexpot!"

"That's me, James! Yes, I'm Sexpot."

Old Soldiers Never Die

(Published in the *Leopard*)

It had been an unusually exhausting day for Stanley, but he was now resting on a perfect white powder puff cloud. Beneath him, Windy Cliffs Golf Course shimmered in the heat. The flags on the greens hung limply and the sailboats out in the bay were almost becalmed.

Inside the gloomy old golf club house the secretary was removing the brass plaque that commemorated record rounds from the wall of the members' lounge, in order for Stanley's name to be added. Stanley's chest filled with pride as his mind savoured each of the sixty-two strokes he had taken to complete his morning round.

Most of the members were sitting out on the sunny balcony sipping afternoon tea or gin and tonics. But his best friends were inside standing at the bar. Hilda, the Ladies' Captain, had her arm round Archie, who was still weeping copious tears. Stanley wanted to jump down to earth just once again to extricate Archie's head from the depths of her voluminous pink angora sweater. But little buds were already beginning to sprout on Stanley's shoulder blades. He was by now almost an angel.

Stanley's last day had started well. He sank a thirty-foot putt at the ninth hole, but then he promptly died.

This wasn't exactly what he had planned. Ten years previously Stanley had fallen foul of the serious disease called the "yipps." (This is when even a four-inch putt refuses to drop into the hole.) Everyone knows what a depressing condition this is and Stanley had been in such low spirits that he had finally admitted to himself and his lawyer that someday he might die....but not until he had played the course like a champion. He had made a will, leaving a considerable fortune to his beloved golf club, a trophy to be known as the Stanley Gordon McTavish Memorial Cup and a request that his ashes were to be scattered on the first tee. (Unfortunately this last request had to be denied because of the prevailing north-east wind and the close proximity of the new dining room extension.)

On that fateful morning our eighteen handicapper stalked his putt on the ninth green from all angles, crouched to get an even better look, fingered his moustache thoughtfully and finally sent the ball rolling smoothly over the grass. It hesitated briefly on a small rabbit dropping, took a little turn to the left and fell into the hole with a satisfying plonk.

The old soldier, despite the heat and his eighty-six years, bent effortlessly to retrieve the ball from the hole and marched off the green in a true sergeant-major fashion. He replaced the putter in the correct section of his old leather golf bag, leaned against Archie's golf buggy and buckled at the knees. Admittedly this was a pose he didn't normally adopt.

Meanwhile, Archie, Fred and George finished the ninth hole in a less spectacular way and prepared to jump into their golf buggies to drive round the hill to the tenth tee. Stanley despised buggies. He always carried his clubs striding smartly in his McTavish tartan plus fours and highly polished golfing brogues, his shoulders back, chest out, as he had first done on the parade ground at Fort George sixty-seven years before.

But this time Stanley did not lead the way round the hill. In fact Stanley was dead to the world and couldn't move from his resting place against the buggy.

Archie said, "I think Stanley's a goner." Without as much as a handshake or a goodbye, thanks for the game, he had indeed gone.... gone to that great golfers' paradise in the sky, not even taking time to arrange his face into a suitable "gone" expression. He looked surprised and outraged, as well he might...having played the best outward nine holes of his entire seventy years as a golfer.

His friends were none too pleased either. They had agreed many years before that nothing, but nothing, would ever interrupt the thrice weekly foursome, not rain, nor snow, (they played with orange golf balls) nor doctor's appointments, not even death itself….at least not without a minimum of three days notice…in writing.

Stanley was now presenting a problem. To carry him back would mean the end of the morning's golf and besides it was the first lovely day of summer and the ladies' section were out in force. Archie was delighted to see that most of them were wearing shorts.

"Look," warned George, "Keep your mind on the problem. Do you think we could put him in the buggy?"

"No," said Fred, "Stanley wouldn't be seen dead in a buggy." But our confirmed old bachelor had enjoyed too many whiskies and cholesterol-ridden steak pies in the golf club. His old ticker had just stopped ticking and he was in no condition to preach to anyone about healthy exercise.

So Stanley was propped up in the buggy, with his old leather golf bag for support at one side and four golf umbrellas at the other.

George jumped into the buggy and followed by Archie and Fred, drove round the bumpy track to the par three tenth tee.

Stanley's head was now lolling grotesquely to the left, his tartan cap had slipped to a jaunty angle and his fingers were trailing the ground. But his unseeing gaze seemed to be fixed on his golf clubs. His driver with the Micky Mouse head cover, a Christmas present from Hilda, was raising itself out of the bag as if some hidden hand was selecting it.

"I think Stanley would like to finish his round," said Fred. But this was going to be difficult because Stanley was now seriously demised with his uncooperative arms getting stiffer and stiffer by the minute.

"I know what we'll do," offered Archie. "We'll take turns to play Stanley's shots with his own clubs. I think this is what he's trying to tell us." He teed up the ball, waggled the club exactly six times, as their old friend had always done, and sent a wonderful shot down the middle of the fairway on to the tenth green. Then George lined up the putt with Stanley's meticulous care and the ball dropped into the hole for a two.

And so the round progressed. As usual the old men miss-hit their

172

shots and their own golf balls rolled into the bunkers or bounced into the bushes, but Stanley's ball, played with Stanley's clubs, always went straight and sweet towards the green. Archie could feel his head being held perfectly still in a vice-like grip as he executed a spectacular shot with Stanley's seven iron and Fred's arthritis eased for a few seconds as he pitched the ball to within two inches of the hole.

Four ladies on a adjacent fairway were puzzled to see Stanley riding in a buggy, and to put it frankly, sprawling in a most unmilitary-like posture, but they waved and shouted the customary "Good morning, gentlemen, lovely day." Stanley usually responded on behalf of all of them. His voice, which had encouraged his soldiers to victory at El Alamein, had never weakened in the intervening years. The club members said that Stanley's whisper could guide super-tankers through the fog, but today he was strangely silent. Instead, George took hold of the lifeless arm by the elbow and raised it up and down as if Stanley were having fun with a yo-yo. It didn't really look like a typical Stanley greeting. Our regimental sergeant major always raised his cap to the ladies. And if he saw the lovely Hilda marching purposefully down the fairway, golf bag on her back and ample breasts bouncing under her pink club sweater, he stood quite transfixed in admiration.

At the end of the round another problem arose. The late Stanley, with a little help from his friends, had played a marvellous round of golf; in fact he had broken the course record. But a scorecard without a signature is null and void and Stanley was past knowing his name, never mind writing it.

From the balcony, the members could see that something very exciting was happening up on the eighteenth green. George and Archie and Fred were standing around the first buggy and there were handshakes and backslaps. In the midst of it all, Stanley seemed to be resting on his laurels and had not yet got out of the vehicle.

No one was prepared for what happened next. Some club members said that Stanley must have seen Hilda blowing him a kiss from the ladies' lounge and what with that wonderful score, had totally lost control. Fred, who knew better, had seen the handbrake move. The golf buggy leapt forward in a very determined fashion, hurtled down the path to the clubhouse and finally toppled into a bed of yellow roses. Stanley and his golf clubs and four umbrellas lay spreadeagled in the flowers. Hilda, knee deep in rose petals, was giving him a vigorous kiss of life and cradling his head in her magnificent bosom.

A scorecard showing Gross Score 62, signed by Fred Watson and countersigned "Stanley G McTavish" in that unmistakable spidery copperplate hand was clutched in his dead white fingers. Stanley's expression of surprise and outrage had changed to a look of pure ecstasy.

As the earthly remains of the new course record holder were removed from Windy Cliffs Golf Course, everybody said what a happy day it had been.

Thirteen

Serious Stories

Holding On With Love

(Published in the on-line women's magazine, The Persimmon Tree)

Changing a king-size duvet cover is like putting knickers on a hippopotamus.

This vast blue thing with the lemon stripes gets washed and tumble dried every week along with the lemon sheets. There is another duvet cover in the linen cupboard but it doesn't match the curtains. However, I don't think this matters much at the moment, when the bucket, placed conveniently at the side of the bed, would lower the tone of the most elegant bedroom. "The bedding looks rather crumpled," I said, "But life's too short to iron king-size duvet covers." My tongue works independently from my brain sometimes.

While the overfilled washing machine shudders and groans in protest, I'll prepare your bath. For the last few weeks, this has been one of the few highlights of the day, so I'll make it special. Then I'll say, "Come, my lady Jennifer, your bath awaits you," and I'll light the candles left over from Christmas, warm the bath towel, and you can soak your poor sweaty body in rose scented suds. That's the easy bit. This week, at the end of the fifth chemotherapy treatment, has been the most difficult yet. Putting on your jeans and a pretty sweater instead of going back to bed is an effort but you admit that it makes you feel better. The Macmillan nurse is so willing to help but you always say to her, "Kate and I will manage, won't we Kate?"

I've been managing for two months now, at first reluctantly. When David asked me to care for you during this awful illness, I didn't hesitate. I couldn't, could I? There was no-one else. So I agreed to give up my real life for as long as I was needed. But it wasn't for you, not at first. I was doing it for my handsome gifted golden boy whose heart was breaking. Nothing in life hurts so much as the hurt to your child…. even if he is 40 and heads a workforce of 800.

In twelve years, I had never really got to know you. When we met, which wasn't very often, we were always polite to each other but we had little in common. You weren't an ordinary girl with an ordinary profession like teaching or nursing. You were a chartered civil engineer. Just imagine it, a slim, blonde beauty in the macho world of the construction industry. David enjoys telling the story of how you and he met on a building site in a thunderstorm. You were wearing a yellow hard hat and a mud-splattered florescent jacket and trousers several sizes too big and he thought you were the most beautiful woman he had ever seen.

Certainly we were never going to be a cosy pair shopping together and swapping recipes. And I had given up any hope of becoming a grandmother. You and David didn't seem to need anyone else in your busy lives…which just goes to show how wrong I was. You were having infertility tests when the cancer was first discovered.

But I don't think I was wrong about your mother. The only time I met Rosalind was at your wedding. Her deep tan, expensive clothes and jingling gold bracelets showed me that life in America with her new husband suited her very well. She said to me, "Kate, I rather like your little frock. Wherever did you get it?" That said it all.

However I'm sure Rosalind would be on the first plane home if she knew just how ill you are. I can't be a substitute for her but we are becoming good friends.

You're dozing but I'll have to rouse you for your 2 o'clock pills. It's taken me ages to learn their names, but now I'm an expert and they trip off my tongue like poetry. There is meto…clo…pramide, and ran…it…idine, clona…zepan and cita…lopram hydrobromide. Their rhythm brings to mind the words of Longfellow :-
> 'Thus it was that Hiawatha
> To the lodge of old Nokomis
> Brought the moonlight, starlight, firelight,

Brought the sunshine of his people,
Minnehaha, Laughing Water,
Handsomest of all the women.'

This week, you can't even concentrate on books or magazines, so sometimes I've been reading to you, mostly the old well loved poems from my schooldays, like 'The Lady of Shallot', 'The Listeners', and, of course, 'The Song of Hiawatha'. Often you close your eyes and I stop reading. But you say, "Go on, Kate," and I read on until you sleep.

Angie has phoned to say that she will be late because her car has broken down. You shake your head in mock exasperation. Angie is an expert in three things, whizzing round the house with a vacuum cleaner, dusting record breaking slaloms round the ornaments with only the occasional breakage, and finding excuses not to come at all.

For a healthy girl, Angie has a worrying number of 24-hour flu bugs and emergency dental appointments, and we wonder what she will think up next. You said you were tempted to ask for a sick note from her mother and I made you laugh at some of the old chestnuts from my teaching days. "Dear Teacher, Angie has been under the doctor with her leg," and "Dear Teacher, Angie vomited up the High Street so I kept her in bed." I have discovered that laughter is a medicine you like to take often.

In between the first three chemotherapy treatments, you still had your good days. Your last one was on the 12th of February and it was an amazing day. You didn't once throw up into the bucket and the awful lethargy had gone. I thought I had wakened from a nightmare and everything was going to be fine after all. The snow was on the ground but the sky was clear blue. You said, "Let's go out for lunch," and we did! You put your long camel coat on top of your jeans and Bob the Builder pyjama top and we sneaked out to the car like a pair of schoolgirls skipping a maths lesson.

"May I take your coat?" said the head waiter at Mortimer's and you replied sweetly, "Not just now, thank you, perhaps later."

"Don't you dare!" I warned as we were led to a table. Your

mischievous smile didn't reassure me and I repeated, "Don't even think about it!" and we were laughing as we settled ourselves, putting the bucket, just in case, tastefully wrapped in a silver and black bag, under the table. Surrounded by ladies who lunch on cottage cheese and cucumber sandwiches, I ordered an omelette and you asked for a plate of chips.

"All our main course lunch dishes are served with boiled potatoes," the haughty waitress said.

"Chips, please," you insisted, "with vinegar and tomato sauce. And two glasses of red wine, please."

You smiled in triumph as she appeared ten minutes later with the chips in a silver salver and the ketchup, not in the vulgar sticky bottle, but in a silver sauce boat. You took only a sip of your wine, but for someone who has the appetite of an anorexic stick insect, you ate with gusto. Then, arm-in-arm, and carrying the bucket, thankfully not required, we paid the bill and fled out to the car park. All the way home, we sang loudly, but off key, to my favourite ABBA CD and arrived at the door in giggling hysterics.

Since then, I think you've deteriorated as each successive chemotherapy session has taken its toll and your laughter tonics are fewer.

But we're holding on. We take each day as it comes and try to make the best of it. Yesterday you cried "Kate!" with some urgency, "Quick!" There at the seed feeder was a bird with red cheeks, a black and white head and golden wing feathers. I searched through the birdie 'Who's Who' and identified it as a goldfinch. We enjoyed its exotic beauty for fully ten minutes before it flew off.

I had thought long and hard about what to give you for Christmas this year, as I did every year. No matter what I finally chose, La Belle Rosalinda's present from America was always bigger, better and more expensive. Ah, but this year, *I* won! She sent you gold earrings which have never been out of the box. I gave you bird feeders, and 'Garden Birds of Britain' which sits by your chair in the sun lounge. Neither of us could tell a coot from a canary in December but now we can pick out a dunnock in a flock of sparrows. Aren't we a smart pair?

You didn't seem interested in much today. We got stuck with the *Scotsman* crossword which we usually manage to complete between us in half an hour. Actually, I read out the clues and you always get the answers before I do. But, this morning, 12 down, 'die of cold' (3,4) had us stumped and you gave up rather quickly, I thought.

The goldfinch appeared again and pecked at the seeds for a minute or so. But Dr Scott stayed a long time. As he was leaving he asked me how I was coping and I said that we were holding on meanwhile. But I am now trying to clutch at tiny, wispy straws which, I fear, blew away in a gale force wind a long time ago. I think I have only two cards left to play.

I've been buying a lottery ticket every weekend when I go home and I always choose our special numbers. When I win three million pounds David and I will go on the Internet and we'll scour the world for cancer specialists. Time may be getting short so they'll all have to come over in private jet planes and fast taxis. One of them will bring over a tiny bottle of the juice of a rare plant found only in the Amazon jungle. They'll combine their knowledge and expertise, add a little this and that to the juice and miraculously, after only two teaspoonfuls, your tumour will be gone.

But meantime, I had to try out plan B. When you were dozing on the couch, I went into the garden and had a straight talk with God. "Why our Jenny, God, why Jen? What has she ever done to deserve this?" I said. "Now if you were to make her well again, I'd know you were a merciful God. And I'll tell the whole world, God, honest I will. My, how the news will spread. All your empty churches will be full again and it will be standing room only. How's that for a bargain, God? Do you hear me, God? Just do it now, God. Make our Jenny's cancer disappear."

I returned to the house to find you distressed because you hadn't quite managed to reach the bucket.

I cried, "I'll take that as a 'no' then, shall I, God?" A great wave of pity for you and for myself swept over me and I sobbed in your arms. You held me until my tears stopped.

"That's all you were needing, Kate," you said. "Just a hug." You are a great believer in the healing properties of a hug. I confessed about my one-sided chat in the garden and you kissed my cheek and said, "I love you, you daft old thing. I thought you'd started talking to the tulips." So, once again, our tears turned to laughter.

Until the last course of chemo is over in two weeks' time Dr Scott has decided to change your anti-nausea medication. So that's yet another pill for me to pronounce. David has been away for two days, but he got back this evening. He is now busy working on his laptop and has forgotten the time, so I'll make a start with the bedtime medication. First the horse-pill size pan drops, then the orange and yellow plastic torpedoes, the two red Smarties, followed by the boring little white ones and lastly the dreaded morphine syrup which you hate. I will you to keep it all down. "Deep breaths, Jen," I urge, "Pretend it's just sweet sherry and drink some more water. That's it!"

David comes running with the bucket, but you're in control now and you relax against the pillow.

"Ice cube, Kate," you say, rather smugly, "The crossword, 'die of cold', it's ice cube." I'm suddenly aware that you haven't given up.

I kiss her. "Sleep well, clever clogs," I say, and I leave you and David in the bedroom together.

I don't like to see you lying in a crumpled bed. I'll ask Angie to iron the duvet cover tomorrow.

Requiem for Danny

(one of my first ever serious stories)

Shirley

"Jason, come here when yer tellt!" The woman's shout broke the silence and heads turned in disapproval. Shirley cursed under her breath as the boy ignored her and continued to rattle the door handles of the waiting funeral cars. Shirley's back was aching, her feet were cold in the grubby white stilettos and under the thin anorak, the pink leggings were slipping down beneath her swollen belly.

She should have gone into the service with the other mothers, if only to take the weight off her legs. But what if Jason started to clamber over the pews or yelled some of his choicest phrases to the congregation? Of course, as she told anyone who would listen, his bizarre behaviour wasn't her fault. The psychiatrist said that Jason had some sort of behaviour disorder and had even prescribed pills which she mostly forgot to give him.

She lost interest in what her son was doing because the church door opened and they were coming out. She craned her neck for a better view and turned to a young woman who was attempting to quieten a squalling baby. "God knows why she wanted to foster him at her age. She must be in her mid forties at least."

A feeding bottle was shoved into the baby's mouth and it sucked greedily. "You get good money for fostering these days. They say she gave up a good job to look after him."

Shirley lit a cigarette. "There's other ways of makin' money. Anyway, she was intendin' to go back to work, I heard. All I know is she kept sending the scabbie faced wee brat to school 'til just a

182

few weeks ago."

The young mother spoke up. "My Billy says that Danny was a nice wee boy."

Shirley's pasty white face contorted in anger. "What's bloody nice about a kid with AIDS? But they didnae tell us, did they? And that bitch Baxter made my son sit beside him. Said he would be a good example for my Jason. Good example! He used tae shit himself, the dirty wee bastard."

The baby had fallen asleep and the girl put the bottle in her pocket. "Right enough, the teachers must've known from the start that he had AIDS."

"I'll bet they did! Took their time tae tell us though, didn't they? And just look at them. Half the bloody staff are at the funeral, the effin' hypocrites." Shirley attempted to mimic Helen Baxter in a high pitched voice. "We appreciate your concern, but we have a very high level of hygiene in our classrooms and toilets and there is ab-sol-utely no cause for panic.....Bitch, I'll sue her for millions if anything happens to my Jason."

Shirley stared with contempt at the tall, smartly dressed woman being helped from the church. "Just look at her. What a bloody carry on to make. He was only a foster kid, for Christ's sake. Nae like yer ain flesh and blood, is it?"

She patted her stomach and hitched up the leggings. She smiled to herself and contemplated once again just how beautiful and well behaved this baby would be. When she was with Kevin, Jason's no-good father, she fantasised about the handsome blond Lars.

"Condoms," he had said in his sexy, sing-song Swedish accent, "Iss like vashing ze feet viss the socks on, ja?" and they had laughed and laughed. Kevin had been locked up in Saughton Prison for a month so Lars had stayed all night and paid her well although the bank gave her less than she had expected for the thick wad of kröne notes.

The crowd fell silent as they watched the small flower bedecked coffin being placed in the hearse.

Shirley yelled again, "Jason, come here, ye wee bugger," and this time the boy returned to his mother's side.

Joanna stood in the doorway on the other side of the street. She was shivering violently, her chin partly hidden in the pink nylon anorak she had stolen from a market stall, her hands deep in the pockets of her torn jeans.

She noticed the pregnant woman struggling with the boisterous child. She watched the small coffin being carried out of the church, but still the tears would not come. Reluctantly she allowed suppressed memories to come flooding back.

They had been quite kind to her in the hospital on that occasion, she remembered.

"Push! Push! Give it all you've got! Just one last push, you can do it. Well done, Joanna! It's a wee boy. You've got a son, my dear."

The nurse laid the baby in her arms. He was the most beautiful creature she had ever seen. Joanna studied the long fingers and the deeply frowning brow and remembered an almost forgotten face from her early childhood. She stroked his damp hair, she kissed his tightly shut eyes. For a few minutes she felt an overpowering love for this tiny person.

"I'm sorry, my dear. Remember the arrangement. I've got to take him away now. I told you he would need some attention in the Special Care Unit." Joanna held the baby closer. "Come on, Joanna, you must give him to me now. He'll be alright…you're only making it harder on yourself, love. Let me take him, there's a good girl."

"He's not a 'him'! His name is Daniel, you bitch, Daniel, do you hear me, Daniel, Daniel! Tell these people his name is Daniel," but the nurse was already wheeling the cot out into the corridor.

She stared at the window of the small side ward. It was very quiet in the hospital now, and it would be dark soon. Flakes of snow were falling gently. An early winter. She covered her face with her skinny punctured arms, and the tears came, soft and quiet at first, like the snow. Then she heaved her exhausted body round and cried great racking sobs into the pillow.

She had not wept since. She had survived for five years, existing from fix to fix, five cold years, her emaciated body never really warm even on summer days. Five years of pain and sickness and hospitals and doorways, each day being much the same as any other.

Punters had plenty of choice amongst the increasing number of prostitutes working in the red light areas of Edinburgh. 'Clean' girls now worked in licensed premises masquerading as massage parlours. The proprietors took their cut but the girls were relatively safe. Some worked the streets because they liked to be independent but they only went with regulars. Joanna had no choice and took desperate risks. But even drunks and perverts viewed Joanna's skeletal body with suspicion and it was becoming more difficult to earn enough to feed her deepening addiction.

The anti-retroviral drugs, when she remembered to take them, were preventing her HIV from developing into full blown AIDS. She knew it would be the heroin that would kill her in the end. In her lonely twilight world there were no real friends, no one to help her or confide in. She never allowed herself to feel the deep black hole in her heart. The heroin kept her safe from painful memories.

The sky was darkening. The hearse rolled silently past her. The good looking woman in the first car glanced at her and for a moment their eyes met.

The wind was getting up and snow was blowing horizontally into the doorway. Joanna turned away, the tears and the snow flakes blurring her vision.

"Goodbye, my wee Daniel," she whispered and disappeared into the gloom of another early winter.

Kate

Alec held her hand as they left the church and helped her into the car. The minister had spoken about understanding and compassion, but Kate was deep in her own private grief and his words were distant. She knew that she was not mourning for Danny only. Her mind trawled through the years of her marriage. The tears were also for all these wasted years when her longing to conceive had turned into an overpowering obsession.

She had stopped having her break with the girls in the office. Even so, she always heard them, "Oh, Jane, what wonderful news! When is it due?" or, "We're getting married next week, just a very quiet affair, you know...."

Then they brought their new babies into the office to be cuddled and admired by the young secretaries but she always made some excuse not to join them. She knew that behind her back they called her stuck-up and cold. When she was appointed office manager in charge of thirty staff, it was because she could be relied on,..... relied on not to have days off with morning sickness or a need to rush home for a domestic emergency.

And poor Alec, poor long suffering Alec, what he had put up with, the violent mood swings, the embarrassing tests, the avoidance of any friends with babies. He had every excuse to leave her, but dearest Alec, it was he who had first suggested fostering.

The probing interviews of the home study were an invasion of privacy and the preparation group meetings went on for weeks, but Alec and Kate persevered, always interested and enthusiastic. They learned about the practical problems of caring for a baby who was HIV positive and they were prepared as well as anyone could be for the emotional problems of loving someone whose future is uncertain. They were also aware of the ignorance and prejudice they might encounter. But at the end of it all, they went to the hospital to collect Danny.

The baby's arrival changed everything, and Kate felt complete at last. Doctors and social workers were delighted at how Danny was thriving. Basking in the attention of his loving foster parents, he grew from an adorable baby and mischievous toddler to an intelligent little boy ready and eager for school.

A few weeks into his first term, Danny began to miss days at school, with a cough and a rash, then occasional diarrhoea. He did not understand why he was ill or the hostility of his classmates and the mothers at the school gate. Mrs Baxter encouraged him to come to school on his good days but he was miserable and clung to Kate for reassurance.

At the end of October, Danny's condition deteriorated rapidly.

The highly potent antibiotics were unable to fight the massive infection in his body. His immune system shut down and Danny was admitted to hospital.

Kate had prayed, "Please God, let my wee Danny live," but within days Danny was almost unrecognisable, his stomach grossly distended and bruised, his face grey, unable to speak, and his eyes terrified. Kate and Alec barely left his bedside as he slipped in and out of consciousness.

The time came when Kate knew that her prayers had not been answered. She held Danny's hand and whispered, "You're going to leave me and Daddy for a wee while, my pet. Your new bike will be there, and, yes, we'll take the rest of your toys in the car and Teddy Hamley is in bed here beside you. We'll see you again very soon, my sweetheart, I promise." He seemed satisfied with that and attempted a smile with dry encrusted lips. A few hours later, she took the tiny ravaged frame in her arms for the last time. "Go towards the light, my angel," she whispered. He relaxed against her breast and his pain was over.

The young mothers were trying to be kind now. They didn't know what to say. Some attempted pious platitudes, "Time will heal." "Poor Danny, poor little soul, it's a mercy, really." "This time next year, you will have come to terms with it." Others stood silently in the background, arms protectively round their children. Her former boss embraced her, "Kate, my dear friend, I know this is neither the time nor the place, but you will phone me when you are ready to come back, won't you?"

She looked out of the car window. Flakes of snow were blowing in the wind. She saw a thin girl huddled in a doorway. She glanced at the pregnant woman with the boy and the other young mother nursing her baby. She felt nothing. No envy. No hurt.

Alec took her hand. "Are you all right, love?"

She returned the pressure of his hand. "Yes, my darling, I'll be fine....we'll both be fine," and she sank back in her seat as the car moved slowly away from the church.

Fourteen

Other Amusing Articles

Three Go Off To Camp

(Winner of the Marty Duncan Trophy at the SAW Annual
Conference March 1997 and published in the Scottish Home And
Country magazine June 1997)

My husband was incredulous. "Camping!" he laughed, "Your idea of roughing it is to sleep in a three star hotel in Skye without an electric blanket. And when you get bitten by midgies, your lumps and blisters look like bubonic plague. And you'll miss Coronation Street!"

However off we went, the three of us, Doris, Moyra and me. This was the first euphoric week of our retirement, having been released from a lifetime in the world of education and we felt game for anything.

The car rocked with our lusty singing. "There was Liz, Liz, drinking the Buck's fizz, in the store….." Perhaps the refrain of the old Girl Guide song was more appropriate, "My eyes are dim I cannot see, I have not brought my specs with me." We were lost and we were only two miles out of Edzell. My husband had insisted that we took map and compass. But our skills were barely at foundation level and we hadn't even passed the test for putting the map together again in the original folds. And what was worse, three pairs of reading glasses were in three rucksacks under three sleeping bags and half of Tesco's in the boot of the car.

I thought I was exaggerating slightly when I told everyone we were going camping. A friend had given Doris the loan of a hut in Glen Lethnot, and by "hut" I understood "chalet" as in skiing holidays in Austria…with central heating, a sunny balcony and maybe even a chalet maid?

It really was the sweetest little doll's house of a hut, but a hut it was, without electricity or water. A tiny kitchen with standing room for one only, a living room full of pre-war furniture and mildewed books, and two bedrooms so small, they would not have passed the regulation size for a toilet on a transatlantic flight.

However, recalling out girl guide skills of nearly fifty years ago, we got ourselves organised. Moyra was voted to be the water patrol, collecting kettles of the purest, sparkling H_2O from a spring 300 yards away.

Doris, of course, had to be the cooking patrol. On a single Calor gas ring, Do produced a three course meal which would have sent Lloyd Grossman into ecstasies of culinary verbosity. Her rice pudding in particular was creamy and ambrosial and the strawberry jam stirred through it got our cook full marks for artistic impression.

I was in charge of cooling the wine in the Burn of Calletar, which gurgled only five yards from our front door. I tried not to disturb the little white-breasted dippers as they slithered drunkenly off the wet stones into the burn in search of food, and then hopped back on again, shaking their feathers dry.

I must mention the "unmentionable." As non-flushing toilets go, the chemical loo in the hut was a state of the art, all blue squirting, all disappearing, odourless convenience. But in sheer horror of it needing to be emptied when we were in residence, we went *al fresco* whenever the sheep turned their backs. My dear friend Doris has a blackmail photo of me, nipping behind the trees at the back of the hut, a vision of loveliness in a white satin and lace nightie, red hill walking socks and unlaced climbing boots.

At half past one on the first night I was having trouble with my sleeping bag. When I turned, it spiralled in the opposite direction and I was encased as tightly as an Egyptian mummy. An urgent little voice was heard from the adjacent sleeping bag. "Liz! There's a HUGE spider on the window!"

"Take its name and go to sleep," I yawned, but the pathetic whimperings of the arachnophobe from inside the sleeping bag would have melted the hardest of hearts. Greater love hath no woman than this, than one who gets out of a warm corkscrewed sleeping bag to relocate a spider for a friend.

But next day, the same lady was as cool as burn-chilled Lambrusco when we came upon our first adder in the heather somewhere near the Sheiling of Saughs. My shrieks of terror and repulsion could be heard in the next glen. Descending near the West Burn we encountered three more sunning themselves on a pile of rocks.

"Aren't they beautiful?" enthused Do and Mo, "Look at their perfect markings. For goodness sake, Liz, they're more frightened of you than you are of them. Scared of a sweet little snake....pull yourself together!" But all I managed was to pull up my socks, right up to the knee, and fall in behind them for safety.

Everyone to her own phobia, I thought that night as I said a friendly goodnight to Incy Wincy, who was now back again on Moyra's window. (I was delighted to see that he had grown at least an inch in diameter in 24 hours.) I then carefully turned my sleeping bag inside out....just in case.

We had timed it well. Four sunny carefree days without a glimmer of interest in what was going on in the world beyond the glen, four days of eagles and adders, deer and dippers. But now thunderclouds were gathering in the hills.

The milk was going off and so were we. So with poly bags full of empty tins and muddy socks, three hygienically challenged campers headed home for an early bath.

The Joy of a Born-again Gardener

The day we moved into our new house, I said, "I'm going to take up gardening!" The exclamation mark is fully justified as this statement startled my husband more than if I'd announced my intention to bungee jump off Ben Nevis….naked.

He always had sole custody of the garden in previous houses and I had never ever lifted a finger, my excuses being a career, a family and a nearby golf course. Now I wanted to muscle in on his new, untouched earth and he stood there defending his territory. However, remembering that most of my new passions petered out within weeks, he agreed to let me be assistant gardener in charge of weeding, watering and dead heading. He would, of course, always be head gardener.

Four years on, a beautiful weed-free garden flourishes. Inside the house, the bookcase overflows with gardening books and the furniture needs dusting.

My family call me MGA, Mrs Great Authority. This is because I love the botanical names for plants. The long Latin words trip off my tongue like beautiful poetry, *acer palm…atum atro…purpureum and phila…delphus coron…arius aur…eus.* The family snigger when I tell them how well my *kniphofia triangularis* are growing. "Mum," they say, "They're red hot pokers, for goodness sake."

But although I love the Latin names, some of the common names are quaint and have an interesting history. According to German folk lore, 'forget-me-not' were the last words of a knight who had been picking a posy of these flowers for his lady before he went off to battle. Unfortunately he was standing too near the edge of a fast flowing river and was swept away.

The shape of the silky leaves of lady's mantle was thought to resemble the cloak of the Virgin Mary. The shrub's botanical name, *alchemilla,* reminds us that alchemists of long ago used the plant to cure blood disorders and stem bleeding in childbirth.

Heaven forbid, maybe I am MGA. At the garden centre check-out two ladies were discussing their purchases. "This 'heeb' was only £3.99," said one of them. I had to stop myself correcting her pronunciation and instead I gave her a few tips about keeping her *hebes* happy. The newly converted love to spread the good news.

I speak to my plants and in particular, to my little rowan tree, sorbus Joseph Rock. In the first year, it was skinny and sickly, and had no blossom or berries. Since rowan trees are lucky and ward off witches, I was anxious that it should survive its first winter. I staked it so it was secure in the wind, pampered it like a favourite child, and now it's growing tall and proud. Its autumn colours of red and orange are a joy to behold.

The *choisya ternata* sundance is my favourite shrub because it is so well behaved. It needs little pruning and its bright yellow leaves shine in the dullest winter days. On the other hand, I am not pleased with the *ajuga reptans* which started as a tiny cutting, but whose shiny far-creeping bronze-green leaves are now threatening to come in and carpet the lounge floor.

Watering on a summer evening is a joy. I spray every plant to the *Chorus of the Hebrew Slaves* by Verdi. This is a useful all purpose tune which in the past, I sang while schussing down ski slopes and soothing teething babies.

I often think I'm like Sisyphus. For his misdeeds the gods condemned him to the eternal task of rolling a boulder to the top of a mountain. Only when he reached the top, it rolled back down again. That's how it is with weeding but the never ending job is strangely therapeutic....although I would never confess this to the head gardener.

But gardening is not all sweet peas and perfumed roses. One evening, when I was watering, I noticed something stirring under the *hosta*. On closer inspection, I discovered a gruesome gang of slugs. I recoiled in horror and ran into the kitchen emitting the sort of primal wail only heard in maternity wards. My husband dug in a dish of beer and invited them to have a party and the next morning we found many bloated black bodies, literally dead drunk. Unfortunately dozens of their kinfolk came to the funeral and did not return home, so until we dug up the hosta, we were holding beer'n'burial wakes twice weekly.

My garden is a haven for the furry and the feathered. The latter, with the exception of seagulls and crows, are very welcome, as long as they eat tidily at the bird table, and I turn a blind eye to the blackbird who strips every berry off the rowan tree at the end of October. However, rabbits are banned and so is Sparkle, a white fluffy mass murderer of baby blue tits. The arrogant puss manages to keep just out of range of my garden hose.

Even I can miss a weed sometimes. Our next door neighbour was (I thought) admiring my immaculate garden as he and the head gardener were enjoying a beer at the shed door. "That pink flower looks like a tattie shaw," he said.

"That," I informed him, "Is a *clematis montana grandiflora*," but then I too spotted the alien pink stem amongst the blue flowers.

"Ah!" said my husband, "But it can't be just a *common* potato. It's probably a *kersus pinkus potatus superprimus.*"

I threatened to turn the hose on them if they didn't stop laughing.

Farewell to the Pound

(published in the *Lady* January 2000)

O n the first day of the new century the pound disappeared. But nobody noticed. No, not the pound in our pocket. Those of us who celebrated too long and too well certainly noticed that our money vanished. I mean the other pound, the one that used to go:

> 16 ounces, 1 POUND
> 14 pounds, 1 STONE
> 8 stones, 1 HUNDREDWEIGHT
> 20 hundredweights, 1 TON

I've been able to chant the table of weight for over sixty years. I also know the table of length including the not so well known bit about there being 10 chains in a furlong and 8 furlongs in a mile. All this obsolete information is stored in my poor brain along with other titbits such as the books of the Old and New Testaments..... Genesis, Exodus, Leviticus, Numbers....and this invaluable little ditty, "In fourteen hundred and ninety two, Columbus sailed the ocean blue."

But I digress. From October 1st 1996, it was decreed by the Government Department of Trade and Industry that all prepacked food should be weighed in metric units. Now since January 1st, this has been extended to all food sold loose, like fruit, vegetables, meat, fish and mint humbugs in jars. If you barely noticed and it hasn't changed your life, this was because it arrived with all the clamour of a bat squeak. At that time we had other things to concern us. We were preoccupied with the fear that civilisation would end, all because two digits were missing from the innards of a few old computers.

There were a few anxious phone calls about the disappearance of the pound to the Jimmy Young programme, but it was confirmed that prices wouldn't go up and everybody was satisfied.

Shopping has gone on much as usual, only the dialogue has changed. A purchase in the fish shop now has the following script:

Customer: "A pound of smoked haddock, please."

Assistant: "That's just a little bit over, love. 510 grams to be exact. Is that okay?"

Customer: "Yes, fine, thanks."

You see, whilst the customer is still allowed to say the "p—" word, it is now against the law for the retailer to use imperial units. If caught in this felonious act, the local authority trading standards department will descend on him like a tonne of bricks. (That's the metric tonne, of course, which is 98.3% of the imperial ton.)

There is only one exception. You may, if you have any, weigh your precious metals in ounces troy, a medieval measure which is equal to 480 grains. Grains of what exactly has been lost in the mists of time.

In the States, our American neighbours have no plans to go metric, but they have changed or omitted some of our imperial units to suit themselves. They don't have stones for instance, and you have to do a tricky division by 14 to decide if someone weighing 220 pounds is fat, thin or just right.

American housewives don't bother to get out the kitchen scales. They measure in cupfuls and it seems to work out fine

On their long and arduous journey to the New World, the Pilgrim Fathers must have forgotten how many fluid ounces there were in a pint, so now they have a gallon which is only 80% of our gallon. This, of course, makes their petrol seem much cheaper. And they still use bushels and pecks, for goodness sake! On a fruit farm in Montana last year, I was tempted to buy a bushel of McIntosh Reds but that's, well…an awful lot of apples. Incidentally, the American bushel is a few apples short of the British bushel, which just goes to show that not everything in the States is bigger and better.

Amazingly there were moves afoot to introduce metrication in

Britain at the end of the 19th century, but the Boer War gave Lord Salisbury and his Government something more important to worry about. Even then we were behind the times. One hundred and fifty years before, the French had adopted the logical and scientifically planned metric system, and it quickly became widespread throughout Europe. Our system of weights and measures was crude by comparison. Most of it was derived from the human body and from natural surroundings, for example the foot and the furlong or furrow long, the length of a ploughed strip of land.

Imperial units disappeared from school lessons nearly thirty years ago but the rest of us have clung on to them with great tenacity. This has caused great confusion to anyone under the age of thirty-five. A Saturday boy at the 'deli' counter in the local supermarket was reported to have cut a whole Stilton into four pieces. The large chunk cost his customer nearly all her pension when in fact she had asked for a mere quarter (of a pound)—or four ounces.

In 1971 decimalisation was introduced and there were massive protests. Even now, some people still speak fondly of the shilling and the half crown and blame all the ills of the country on their demise.

But there has never been much of an outcry about the slow disappearance of our tables of length, area and volume. They were much too complicated and only people whose teachers believed in prolonged chanting ever mastered them. Officially we are metric and it is a hanging offence for manufacturers and retailers to use the old units. The rest of us muddle along with both systems. We buy twenty square metres of carpet for a floor which has always been fifteen feet by twelve feet and we paint the walls with a four-inch brush using two litres of emulsion. We can have a pint of milk delivered to our door only if it is in a returnable bottle, but if we buy milk at the supermarket, it's got to be in litres. My twin granddaughters officially weighed in at 2270 and 2500 grams, but the metric police weren't around and the nurse whispered that at 5 and 5½ pounds they were just perfect.

However, the government has no plans to change our road traffic signs, meanwhile. They probably thought about it, but discarded the idea as being too disruptive and expensive. Marathon runners now have to suffer forty-two kilometres, farmers have to measure their fields in hectares; but they've left the rest of us with our miles.

So although the British Imperial System has crumbled and nearly everything has officially changed, everything really remains the same. We can buy a pint of beer in the pub and get fined if we drive at over 70 mph on the motorway.

And one thing is certain, the taxman will always demand his pound of flesh.

Cold Comfort

(This little piece was second in a club competition.)

The medics say that you catch the common cold when you travel in crowded trains in February. Not in my case. The nasty little virus catches *me* whenever I want to look my best at events such as parties or weddings.

The medical dictionary dismisses the common cold as a mild viral infection lasting three or four days. The colds I take are of the uncommon variety. Even when I pamper them with paracetemol, blackcurrant soothers and hot whisky toddies (and I can recommend the latter) my cold lasts for two weeks. Unpampered, it lasts the same time.

The first symptom is an uneasy shivery feeling as the wee germ searches for a nice place to settle. A generous whisky toddy gives me a blissful night's sleep, but in the morning I feel as if I have swallowed a hedgehog. Sadly I will not have developed that husky croak which prompts folk to say, "You poor soul, you should be home in bed."

Next the bug moves onwards and upwards to the eyes and nose. This is truly the antisocial part of the illness, the scourge of romantic dinners. For who can stare lovingly into streaming bloodshot eyes or enjoy avocado mousse when the person sitting opposite is blowing the contents of her skull into scores of man-size tissues. And talking about tissues, have you noticed that this same tiny square multiplies itself twenty-fold if it finds its way into the washing machine?

At the end of this stage, old herpes, the cold sore, appears in its usual place, stretching from the upper lip to under the nose.

Nothing can be done about this unsightly, painful blister, which makes me a party pariah and out of the kissing game for another two weeks.

A few days later, the cold gets bored with me and looks for fresh mischief elsewhere. It leaves behind a tickly cough that makes the minister glower at me from the pulpit and half the congregation pass pan-drops along the pew. It's the kind of cough that starts immediately I turn off the light and my nearest and dearest having tholed stages one, two and three, finally departs to the spare bed.

Some people, usually of the male variety, describe these symptoms as a 'touch of the flu.' Well, let me tell you, the flu doesn't *touch* you. A lumberjack attacks your head, a gang of Spanish Inquisitors jump on your joints and your thermostat travels from the Sahara to Siberia in the matter of minutes. That's influenza!

These hypochondriacs have only caught the common cold…just like me.

Pensioner On The Piste

(Published in the Scottish Home & Country December 1998)

W hat do you do when the man in your life was born at the time of the third Winter Olympics and whose favourite footwear is not his slippers, but his ski boots, with a pair of Blizzards attached?

And what do you do if he won't leave you home alone now that you have retired from the world of work? On the other hand, he is going off with his ten ski-mad friends to pay annual homage to the French Alps.

The day after I agreed to go with them (only to make up the number for a full chalet discount) my husband, fearful that I might chicken out, lured me to the ski shop.

There in return for a large chunk of my pension, I was kitted out with "ultra-light" boots which I could barely lift off the floor, the latest in parabolic skis and all the rest of the paraphernalia required for sliding down snowy mountains.

The venue was Courcheval, which, not being a skier, I had never heard of. Getting mildly into the spirit of things, I did a little pre-holiday homework. Courcheval, according to the brochure, is a ski resort at four different levels, 1300, 1550, 1650 and 1850 metres and is the most sophisticated of the Trois Vallées, a vast snow area which offers endless possibilities for all grades of skier.... including retired ladies who, up until now, had never even watched *Ski Sunday*.

Weather conditions prevented me having any pre-holiday practice in the Lecht or Glenshee, but I prepared in every way. Each day I put on my ski boots and skis and stomped about the front hall. I studied ski books and videos from the library and did some snow ploughs on the carpet. I carried my skis around the house on my right shoulder, tips pointing forward in the correct manner. (The postie who saw me through the window on more than one occasion thinks I am two postcards short of a delivery.)

We arrived at Courcheval 1300, or Le Praz, as the original village is called, just as the setting sun was casting dark lavender shadows on the pistes and above, the mountain tops looked like giant scoops of strawberry ice cream. Floodlights illuminated the Olympic ski jump opposite our chalet and young champions were leaping high and long into the starry sky. At last I could feel the magic of it all and I was looking forward to my debut in the morning.

We went for an after dinner stroll through the village. The bars and the popular little créperies were busy but the narrow winding streets were quiet. Courcheval 1300 is for serious skiers who want to get to bed early to dream of sunny pistes and perfect turns.

I had booked in advance with ESF, Ecole du Ski Français. For 700 francs (about £70 at the current rate of exchange) I was to get three hours of tuition daily for a week, in a group of no more than ten pupils.

My first day began badly. Of all the people congregating at Courcheval 1850 for the start of the morning's skiing, I was the one chosen by a malevolent black mountain chough on whom to deposit the entire contents of his digestive system…. on my shoulders, sleeves and woolly hat. Further depression descended when I noticed a tiny three-year-old whizzing past with his instructor. He was the complete skier, little Disney suit, minute skis, goggles, lift pass hanging round his neck…. and a large purple dummy in his mouth.

The beginners' class was to be shared between two instructors. Nothing in Jules' face gave the impression that he had been lying awake savouring the anticipation of taking his new class. He ran an arrogant, unfriendly eye over yet another bunch of graceless, clumsy novices, hovered particularly on my choughly soiled chain store suit and my retired face and announced that I should be in Fabian's group along with three others. Although I was the oldest, Keith, Emma and Mary had seen more snowy winters than the young confident group which Jules chose.

Fabian (say his name in your best French accent) was a lovely young man, patient, helpful and genuinely interested in our progress. For the rest of the week the four of us were inseparable as we learned to ski together.

We started by side stepping up the slope which was as exhausting as swimming up a waterfall. We learned to balance and control our speed by snowploughing. We hopped on and off the bubble cars and button tows like experts.

Within a few days I was carving near perfect turns down the gentle green runs. I had found my ski legs. I would be writing fiction if I said I was always vertical and always in control, but my falls were usually gentle with only minor bruising on a well padded part of my anatomy.

In spite of my progress and enthusiasm, my husband warned against afternoon skiing when my legs were tired and the snow was getting slushy in the bright sunshine.

So he and I used our lift passes to wander higher than any of our chalet companions. We picnicked at Saulire at 2738 metres and photographed Mont Blanc; we sipped a glass of wine at Verdon; We shouted "hup, hup, hup" to the dozens of would-be Alberto Tombas at the slalom races at Méribel.

At glitzy exclusive Courcheval 1850, where the rich arrive by private plane, I window-shopped and indulged in my favourite pastime of studying people.

In the many quality shops the ski and après ski wear had price labels like telephone numbers but the jewellery had no vulgar tag at all. What the heck, if you need to ask the price, you can't afford it.

Up here are the designer stubbled gorgeous guys who have skied the slopes long enough to get a mahogany tan. Then there are the jet-setters who hang about outside the cafés with mobile phones and fancy skis they never actually put on. The women are straight out of glossy fashion magazines. They wear Gucci sunglasses, golden yellow ski-suits, silver fox snoods and perfectly applied carmine lipstick. They greet the handsome princes of the piste with hugs and air kisses.

On the ride up to Verdon we shared our bubble car with a Sloan Ranger type who talked loud ski techno-babble about the torsional rigidity of his new skis....and proceeded to wobble his way down a green run with far less skill than me. I felt rather smug.

I do not have the courage to be more ambitious with my skiing. The mogul fields with their large "boomps" and the near vertical drops of the black runs are my kind of nightmare. But leave me under a brilliant blue sky with soft powdery snow on my boots and I'll make my slow but stylish descent with a huge smile on my face.

From now on I'll be going over the mountains but I won't be over the hill.

Crazy about Crosswords

(published in the *Leopard* April 2002)

I'm a member of the north-east branch of C.A....Crosswords Anonymous, that is. Friends and family know about my problem and smile indulgently. They do their best to divert my attention to all the other joys of retired life. But let me within a pencil's length of a square grid and I can't help myself.

I'm allowed to have the crossword in bed for a whole hour in the winter and a quarter an hour in the summer before my husband pushes me into the shower. I have never completed the puzzle by then, (can anyone do the crossword in fifteen minutes? Apart from the recently deceased Inspector Morse, that is?) so it niggles in my brain throughout the day. Milk boils over, I forget what I'm in the supermarket for and I walk past my golf ball.... all because 10. Down has got me stumped. Crosswords are seriously affecting my life.

By definition, a crossword addict is someone who buys a newspaper and doesn't even look at the headlines. That's me. A second or two to admire the beautiful half symmetry of the black and white squares and then I dive into 1. Across with all the urgency of a hopeless junkie.

It all started when I was plastered from hip to toe after a skiing accident. Completely immobile, I was becoming a world authority on TV soaps. I needed an intellectual challenge. I remember my first cryptic clue. I was turning over the pages of the *Leopard,* too uncomfortable to read even the shortest article, and I glanced at the crossword. "Takes out another policy, but gets better. (8 letters.)" "RECOVERS," I thought and counted out the letters on my fingers.

I was so pleased with myself—but it was the only clue I managed. The rest were gobbledegook. I gave up, I would have to wait a month for the answers. But I also solved two clues in the morning paper.

The next morning, I studied the clues along with the solutions and made sense of a few more. By the time the plaster came off I could tackle about half. Then one weekend, with a little help from a friend, I finished the *Scotsman* prize crossword. I thought I was the only person in Scotland who could possibly have done this and waited expectantly (but in vain) to see my name as the winner of the £60 posh pen the following Saturday. I also wanted to phone Peter Bee, the compiler, to say that in spite of his devious cunning I had his measure.

But countless people do crosswords everyday, in bed, on the train, during a tea-break, in the pub, in fact anywhere and at any time. The very first crossword appeared in the New York Sunday paper *The World* and a few years later, in 1924, a crossword was published in the *Sunday Express*. By the thirties almost every daily and Sunday paper had succumbed to the new craze. One spoilsport clergyman wrote to complain that the little squares were a menace, making inroads on the working hours of all classes.

At first most of the clues were synonyms, the type of puzzle which today we call the Quick Crossword. This is now considered to be rather lowbrow since it is easily completed with the help of a dictionary. The cryptic crossword, on the other hand, can be absolutely mind bending with clues which are punned, ruthlessly distorted and falsely punctuated. But at the end, the solver should be able to say, "Got it!" and be able to justify his answer. For example, the crossword in the December issue of the *Saga* magazine (which makes no concessions for the ageing brains of its readers) had this clue. "Adversary lacking my bearing." (4,5,4 letters) If the setter had wanted to be kind, he might have slipped in a few commas. But this is how it works out: - adversary …ENEMY…subtract MY… ENE…giving the bearing EAST NORTH EAST. Clever, eh?

You have to learn to think laterally, because the setter pretends to be saying one thing, but actually means something completely different. He takes great pleasure in leading you down false paths. 'A Scottish flower, (3 letters)' should not have you searching through a botanical encyclopaedia. You see, to the twisted mind of the setter, a flower is something which flows. Yes, that's right, a river, and in this case, the TAY. Likewise a number is that which numbs so your only problem is how to spell ANAESTHETIC. Eventually clues with bloomer, sewer, tower, etcetera become easy.

Every cryptic crossword has a number of clues solved by anagrams. Some are simple like 'Made out the cheese, (4 letters)' You can surely manage this one?...OK, I'll whisper it, EDAM. Unscrambling thirteen letters to come up with the word XANTHOCHROISM is a bit more difficult.

One further device is the hidden word. Once you know to look for it, the answer to "Cereal harvested from very early times," is easy to spot.

All crossword addicts have a favourite clue. Brevity is the hallmark of a good compiler and 'Die of cold, (3,4 letters)' with its clever solution ICE CUBE is as neat as they come.

When I first started doing crosswords I had none of the tools of the trade. You would have to be the most erudite of the literati not to need a little assistance. Since I need all the help I can get, I have a huge arsenal of books including dictionaries, *Roget's Thesaurus, Chamber's Anagrams* and *Collin's Complete Crossword Companion*. My favourite is *Cassell's Crossword Finisher,* which I got for 20p in a jumble sale. How anyone could have discarded this invaluable little gem, I can't imagine. I use it every day. It's the book I'll choose when I am marooned on a desert island. (Assuming of course, that the paper is delivered every morning.)

My long suffering husband doesn't do crosswords but sometimes gets involved reluctantly. One night in bed, he shouted out "ANNIE," turned over and snored. Now my name isn't Annie and I lay awake drawing up the terms of our divorce settlement. Then I remembered my last words before we switched off the light, "I'm stuck with 'gun getter,' five letters, with 'I' in the fourth place."

Some enthusiasts are determined to finish the crossword to the point of obsession. A few months ago the *Leopard* accidentally published the wrong grid for the given clues. This, of course, made the puzzle impossible and left thousands the length and breadth of the north-east totally bereft for a month…except for one subscriber who completed it by designing a correct replacement grid. His entry included a polite letter to the editor complaining that the *Leopard* crossword was getting "A wee touch too difficult."

I may have a mild addiction, but that's one man with a *serious* problem.

Managing my Mastectomy

(This was the leading article in the new revamped *My Weekly* October 2006. The fee was the most I have ever earned for an article and there were many letters in praise of it in subsequent magazines.)

On the 9th of November, 2005, in the shower room of Ward 10, Ninewells Hospital, Dundee, I said "Bye, bye, boobs," because an hour later, I was to have them both removed, along with all the lymph nodes; because if the cancer is going to spread, this is usually its first port of call.

For many women this is the worst possible nightmare. One woman in the ward actually said she would rather die of the cancer that was in her breast than have a bilateral mastectomy. She was young and pretty and probably newly married to the handsome man who arrived at visiting time with armfuls of flowers. But I was nearly sixty-seven and I didn't feel that way at all. I hadn't loved my breasts for a long time. They were a mismatched pair, too big and too heavy. The left one was heading south and the right one southwest. They required advanced scaffolding in the form of expensive bras to keep them under control and even then, I had at least half a dozen of these ugly over shoulder boulder holders still in their boxes because they were uncomfortable and the straps dug into my shoulders. And now in my right breast there was an invasive lobular cancer Grade 3. Because there is a risk that this type of cancer sometimes reappears soon after in the other breast, my surgeon and I jointly agreed to get rid of both of them. I have never regretted this decision.

I am one of life's greatest cowards. If I had been in the Resistance, I would have confessed everything I knew, and made up lots that

I didn't know, before the Gestapo even started the interrogation. So when I awoke out of the anaesthetic that evening, I couldn't believe that I was in no pain whatsoever. My first thought was that I hadn't been to the theatre yet, but my body under the blanket looked strangely flat. I was hooked up to a morphine supply, which fortunately I never needed, and three drain bottles, one from each missing breast and one from under my arm where all the right side lymph nodes had been. I was up and about the following morning carrying my drain bottles in supermarket bags (apparently no-one has ever invented anything more convenient) and in the five days that followed I became expert in threading the tubes and bottles through the sleeves of my nightdress in order to shower and wash my hair. My ward mates and I held each other's bottles as we did our arm exercises or used the hairdryer. We winced in sympathy when the sudden tug on tender skin reminded us that we had turned over in bed and forgotten about our temporary appendages.

I got home on day six and then the problems started. My stitches were not removed until day thirteen but by then I had developed the first of five seromas, (swellings due to fluid collection) and at one stage I thought my stitches would burst open. Each time my husband and I had to make a sixty mile round trip, twice in horrendous weather, to the hospital to have a needle aspiration by one of the Macmillan breast cancer care nurses. These darling girls were indispensable and I will be eternally grateful for their reassurance and kindness. They said my seromas, the brief shooting pains like electric shocks, my sore stiff arms and the extreme tiredness were all common and would disappear eventually, and they did. I never mentioned my 'phantom' breasts in case they locked me up but for several weeks I felt them bounce in the old way when I ran down stairs and at one stage I was convinced that I had nipple rash. I longed for the security of my old firm control bras but I had thrown them all out weeks before.

To my friends and family I was a star. "How well you have coped," they all said. Only my husband knew how many times I cried and that my confidence had an eggshell fragility. We had both been very stressed since the initial diagnosis and chats and cups of tea at 4am were not uncommon. But nothing was so awful as sitting in the clinic, sightlessly leafing through ancient magazines, with the appointment times running an hour late, waiting to find out the results of the post operative lab tests. We were both visibly shaking with tension. Miraculously, my lymph nodes were cancer free but the margins of the tumour were too close to my breastbone for safety. I escaped chemotherapy but I required radiotherapy and a five-year course of Tamoxifen.

However, as far as bras were concerned, the world was at my feet. My chums and I had fun discussing what size I should be when I got my prostheses. Should I get Jordanesque ones or an average 'C' cup? But I had already made up my mind. I was going to have what I had always wanted. I went off to get my first post operative soft breast forms from my Macmillan nurse, carrying the cutest, laciest, silkiest, creamiest, wispiest size 34A cup bra, purchased from one of a few excellent mail order companies who specialise in mastectomy wear. I felt sad to read, in one of these brochures, that only twenty-five years ago, women who had mastectomies had to stuff their empty bras with chopped up nylon stockings, and their post operative support was negligible. The management of breast cancer has come a long way since then.

Unfortunately it was too early for me to wear even the softest of prostheses and by the time my husband and I reached the hospital car park I decided the bra with its lamb's wool padding was too uncomfortable against my recently stitched skin and had to come off….immediately. So I struggled in the back seat with winter coat and several other layers and my husband obligingly leaned over and helped from the front. Eventually, I emerged from the back of the car carrying the above mentioned wispy garment to find that the car park attendant was getting rather interested in what two old age pensioners appeared to be doing in the car. "Maybe we should explain?" I suggested, but my husband said, "Just let's get out of here!" and in the gloom of a late December afternoon, the attendant shone his torch and noted our number.

Just before Christmas, I attended Ninewells for my radiotherapy planning. This involved about twenty minutes of lying completely still with my right arm raised above my head under a machine called a simulator. This expensive piece of equipment moved around taking X-rays from all angles and the radiographers did complicated mathematics to determine the strength and exact location of the treatment. After their calculations, the two radiographers played noughts and crosses on my chest with a blue marker pen and their results were double checked and confirmed by the consultant radiologist.

The blue markings were very messy. Throughout the course of treatment, the ink rubbed off on underwear, bedclothes and bath towels, but the more it came off, the more the radiographer took the blue pen and cheerfully drew the lines back on again.

The area is also marked out by permanent tattoo marks. I asked if I could have a mountain daisy, a tasteful little butterfly and a love heart, but all that was on offer were three very ordinary blue spots the size of a freckle.

The radiotherapy itself started a week later and on twenty occasions my husband and I again made the sixty mile round trip to the hospital. At first the treatment was a breeze. I slapped on the recommended moisturising cream and every day I did my count down....thirteen zaps down and only seven to go, fourteen down and six to go....and then the effects of these high energy beams hit me. The treated area and in particular, my scars, turned the colour of raw steak. Each zap after that was like sunbathing topless, and without suntan cream, in the noonday sun in Las Palmas in August.... and then going out and doing it again the next day and the next and the next....Even when the treatment was over the radiation continued to cook for two more weeks and all I could do was apply buckets of cream and hunt each day for my softest vests. At this time the common side-effect of the Tamoxifen was kicking in. My hot flushes have been minimal but occasionally I have one which is like Vesuvius erupting and rivulets of molten lava stream down my face and neck.

I never wore my pretty 34A cup bra again until six weeks after the treatment ended, when my Macmillan nurse fitted me with silicone prostheses, which are free to National Health patients. They look and feel rather like chicken fillets and they are very comfortable, more comfortable than my real breasts ever were. I have bought two more glamorous bras, which I love to hang on the washing line. I look good in little T-shirts and polo neck sweaters. My friends swear they can't tell I'm wearing a mastectomy swimsuit when we go to the local baths and my family say my hugs are just as soft as they always were. Scarring and radiotherapy tattoo marks prevent me from choosing anything too plunging but then, décolleté has never been my style. My golf swing, unimpeded by large bosoms, has improved and my drive is twenty yards longer. Such was my joy when I played my first game that I sent my surgeon a card telling him all about it. And when I demonstrate my skipping skills to my twin granddaughters, I am no longer in danger of getting a black eye from bouncing boobs.

As for the cancer, the oncologist says all is fine at the moment. I am giving it my best shot by continuing to lead a very healthy lifestyle. I certainly feel on top of the world and I am so grateful to all those involved in my treatment and recovery. One of my 'get well' cards said,

> "Yesterday is history,
> Tomorrow is a mystery,
> But today is a gift."

And indeed it is.

Plastered

(This article won the Marty Duncan Trophy for the most amusing short article at the SAW Conference in 2008.)

"This is a ruptured medial ligament," boomed the god of Orthopaedics to his students. "It is almost always the result of a skiing accident, when the boot doesn't come out of the binding." He turned his attention from the two pounds of raw mince that was my knee and asked, "Going too fast down the black runs, eh?"

"Something like that," I lied. In fact, I was doing a slow but elegant descent of a green run when a three year old pocket rocket dressed in full ski wear and sucking a large purple dummy, knocked me over. The mother of this miniature Fritz Strobl whizzed past me without stopping.

"Total immobilisation for six weeks," he ordered and swept out with his entourage.

I was wheeled to the plaster room wearing my temporary attire, voluminous NHS shorts which would have been loose on an overweight hippopotamus.

"What colour would you like?" asked the cheery technician and handed me a shade card offering every colour in Joseph's dream coat. He looked truly disappointed when I turned down his suggestion to go for lilac to match the shorts. Call me boring and sartorially unadventurous but I chose to be encased from hip to toe in chalk white to match my pain ridden face.

I discovered that, in plaster, most mundane tasks are impossible. Making tea whilst balanced on crutches is suicidal, putting on knickers requires the arm extension of a chimpanzee and, to mention the unmentionable, going to the loo is more of a miss than a hit, as you and the plaster slip off the seat. To have any chance of success, the manoeuvre has to be initiated a full hour and a half before urgency sets in.

I wasn't the only vulnerable one. My husband fled to the spare bedroom when my ton weight appendage flung itself on to a delicate part as I turned in my sleep. Poor darling, he was singing soprano castrato for a month.

Until the third week, my daily wash consisted of dabs with a sponge on all reachable non-plastered areas. I suspected, therefore, that I was not the sweetest smelling girl on the block. My husband planned the logistics of giving me a bath. The problem of getting me in and out of the tub and what to do with the leg required advanced engineering skills. I was lowered into the bath and my leg, wrapped in black bin liners, was to be supported above the water on an upturned plastic laundry basket. Unfortunately we had forgotten about the Principle of Archimedes. (He was the old Greek mathematician who ran starkers through the streets of Syracuse shouting "Eureka, Eureka!" He had discovered that the bigger the body in the bath, the more the rose scented suds will spill over the edge and flood the bathroom floor.) Meanwhile I had submerged. To his credit, my husband plucked me up from the depths with such a speed that I nearly died of the bends. This exercise was never repeated. Friends and family merely took care to be upwind of me at all times.

As I was becoming a world authority on TV soaps, my darling partner suggested jaunts in the car. But there is no room in a Mini for a plastered leg unless it is propped up on four cushions and hung out the rear left side window.... with a red rag tied to the end.

His next idea was to borrow a wheelchair from the Red Cross. At our first outing I discovered that wheelchairs have no suspension and roads are usually eight teeth-dislodging inches lower than the pavement.

In a wheelchair, you are a non-person. Passers-by chatted to the pusher, they ignored me. "Was she run over by a bus? Will she ever walk again?" they asked. Then they would relate their own medical problems. It seems that everyone in town has had a 'leg' at some time....broken ones, cracked ones, twisted ones and missing ones.

As the weeks went by, the pain disappeared but a new problem developed. Every evening I waited desperately for my husband to come home from work. Before he got his jacket off I was pleading for the bottle-brush treatment to relieve the terrible itch under the plaster. As he squeezed the long prickly brush into the gap at the ankle, I yelled in ecstasy, "Ooooh, aaaah, more, more, up a bit, round a bit, yes, yes, yes!" Our neighbours thought we had discovered something truly wonderful to spice up our long marriage.

If you are powerless in a wheelchair, you are a king on crutches. National Health sticks get you the best table in a restaurant, doors opened and library books carried. And you can take as long as you like crossing the road as motorists have a natural squeamishness about running over those already crippled.

After six long weeks, I was looking forward to seeing my pal in the plaster room, but he was off duty. Instead Cruella DeVil approached wielding a Black and Decker saw. I nearly fainted as I imagined a re-enactment of 'The Texas Chainsaw Massacre' with gory bits littering the plaster room floor. I demanded to see proof of her Standard Grade qualification in joinery. She informed me, rather huffily, that she had never severed a limb....yet. The saw screamed through the plaster, and half a minute later I was blissfully scratching my skinny white leg.

Eventually, after weeks of the torture they call physiotherapy, it was time to have a final consultation with the big man in Orthopaedics. He gave his entire attention to my knee and invited his disciples to feel the 'interesting twang' in the kneecap. He did not speak to me directly but I got the message. "This lady," he said, "Would be ill-advised to ski again."

So, no more stylish descents on these green runs with soft powdery snow on my boots. No more gorgeous ski instructor with his mahogany tan and sexy designer ski suit so tight I could tell which coins he had in his back pocket. No more sundowners on the chalet balcony.

It's enough to make a poor girl get herself.... Well and truly ...... plastered.

Liz Strachan was born in Aberdeen in 1939 and calls herself a "pre-War Baby." She went to school at Aberdeen Academy and then studied Mathematics at Aberdeen University.

She worked for thirty-six years in the teaching profession, which provided fertile ground for her subsequent writing career.

After holding positions in a number of schools across Scotland, she moved to Montrose Academy in 1976 and remained there for the next twenty years.

Her writing career began in 19991 when she won First Prize in a European letter-writing competition. From there she progressed from strength to strength, having her work published in a wide range of magazines and periodicals.

Her first full-length book, *A Slice of Pi,* published in October 2009, deals with Mathematics, still her first love.

This compendium brings together the best of Liz Strachan's essays, short stories, poems, letters and articles. They are funny, entertaining and moving too. There really is something here for everyone, all written in a very enjoyable way.

Liz is now retired from teaching but is still an active writer. She lives in Montrose with her husband Sandy and has two sons.

Liz has asked for the royalties from the sale of this book to go to MacMillan Cancer Support.